STERLING
CALHOUN MEN BOOK 4

KATHI S. BARTON

This is a work of fiction. Names, characters, places, and incidents are products of the author's imagination or are used fictitiously and are not to be construed as real. Any resemblance to actual events, locations, organizations, or persons, living or dead, is entirely coincidental.

World Castle Publishing, LLC
Pensacola, Florida
Copyright © Kathi S. Barton 2017
Paperback ISBN: 9781629896656
eBook ISBN: 9781629896663
First Edition World Castle Publishing, LLC, April 3, 2017
http://www.worldcastlepublishing.com

Licensing Notes

Cover: Karen Fuller
Editor: Maxine Bringenberg

CHAPTER 1

Alta set a plate full of food in front of him, and Sterling stared at it before looking up at her. She'd been with him for nearly four months now, and he was sure that he was about as fattened up as he was going to get. She smiled at him and told him to eat.

"I'm thinking you're either fattening me up for a huge dinner, or you think I'm still skinny. First, I'm not Santa, and second.... Well, second, I'm not that hungry anymore." She patted him on the cheek and walked away as he started putting butter on his pancakes. "Did I tell you that I'm supposed to host Christmas this year? I haven't any idea why I got volunteered. I guess I should pay more attention when they're all talking."

"They do love to talk, your family." He nodded as she handed him a platter of bacon and sausage. "Randal is coming. I think he should be here any second."

The back door opened and there stood his brother covered in snow. He was brushing it off his head as he was telling Alta that he could eat again. When he sat across from him, stealing one of his pieces of bacon, Alta gave him pancakes as well.

"Mom sent me over. And Grandma wants to know if you have enough decorations for Christmas." He said he had some. "I'm also supposed to tell you that once you're ready to start with the decorations, you're to call Mom. She said don't forget. Wanna

5

go shopping with me?"

"No. I have work to do, and Noelle has a list of things she needs me to pick up as well. I guess she's been making some pretty good deals with a few vampires that Noah knows." Randal finished his breakfast before he did, which didn't surprise Sterl. He didn't have live-in help and no one cooked for him. "Why did Mom send you here?"

"Mostly to make sure that you're eating well and that you're not lazing around the house. I haven't any idea why she thinks that, but she told me to see about you. And I think she's still pissed at Grandda. He should have known better than to be late for dinner on Friday." They both laughed. "Did I tell you that I'm interviewing for help at the house?"

"I've got someone coming to your house this afternoon, Mr. Randal. You can hire him or not, but you should know that he's a better cook than I am." Sterl didn't ask, but was glad that Randal did about what the person was. "Witch, and Myra said for you to call her when you have a moment. She wants to talk to you about something."

"I can do that." While they discussed how to get in touch with the witch, Sterl zoned out. He really did have a list of things to do today, and most of it had nothing to do with the things he had to pick up for Noelle.

They were business partners. Mostly he worked upstairs in her antique shop, but when she wanted someone to come along with her on buying trips, or to lift heavy things, he went to take care that she didn't lift much. Noelle was having twins in the early spring and everyone watched over her.

The thing on his list that he had tried to avoid for several weeks now was the meeting with his grandma. She told him if he bailed on her today that she'd tell everyone his secret. He was sure that most of them knew that he painted, but the rest of his secret was something he was afraid of them finding out.

He was afraid that Joe knew already, and that she was in on this whole thing with him having a gallery opening. Sterl wasn't ready for that. He had been working a great deal, painting whatever popped into his head, but he'd not shown anyone his work except his grandma. And only then because she'd barged in and simply pulled out his canvases and looked for herself.

"You need this as much as I do." He told Grandma that he didn't need it. "Yes, you do. You need for people to sit up and take notice of you. You're very talented, and I for one cannot wait to see what others say about you."

"They're not going to care. And if they do, I can't imagine that their words would be kind." She smacked him on the back of his head. "Grandma, you know that I'm telling you the truth. I've had no formal training other than a few classes at the YMCA when I was a kid. I like painting because it's relaxing to me. I don't want someone to tell me it's crap."

"No one had better tell you it's crap." He laughed at her tone. "All right, I did walk right into that one, but they're going to love you as much as I do. And if you find yourself a mate, I'm sure she'll love it as well."

And now, today as a matter of fact, he was going with Grandma to talk to a person who owned a gallery willing to show his work. This man, Sullivan, was a friend of the family, she'd told him, so he was sure this was happening because of that and not his talent. Or the lack of it. Sterl wasn't looking forward to this any more than he was decorating his house for Christmas. His heart, he thought, just wasn't into it.

After Randal left, he went up to change. He was wearing a suit for this meeting, but bringing some jeans to wear afterwards when he went to pick up some furniture. He was going out the door when Myra was suddenly standing in front of him.

"It's today." He nodded, then realized that he had no idea what she was talking about. "Remember when I told you that

7

someone was coming, a male?"

"Yes. You said they were going to come to mean a great deal to me. I've been thinking about what you said, and I'm not sure about this." She asked him why not. "I have no idea, but I'm still a little skittish around people, and I'm not sure that I could handle someone else in my life right now when I don't even have my own set."

"Sometimes life gives you little bumps to keep you on your toes." He told her that he wasn't ready for bumps, little or large. "You'll be fine. Also, I wanted to tell you about the gallery opening that you're going to have. It's going to be epic, and the Bentleys want to go to it when you're all set up."

He started to ask her how she'd found out, but decided that he didn't want to know. Instead, he grabbed his coat and made his way to his car. Sterl was slightly afraid of Myra and the Bentleys, but didn't say anything. When Myra was seated in his car when he started it up, he looked over at her.

"I don't know what's going to happen with the gallery." She said that she did. "Well, don't tell me. I'm not sure I want any disappointment right now."

"Why do you believe you'll be disappointed? Never mind. I can see it in your heart. You're very talented, young man. And as your grandmother says, it's time you let the world know it." He backed out of the garage and pulled into the busy street in front of his house. "Will you at least promise me that when you have it set up you'll let me know?"

"Since I'm sure that you know the answer to that, I'm not going to say. I'm supposed to meet my grandma in an hour. Are you going as well?" She told him that she was too busy today, but would sometime soon. "Good. And if you have a few minutes, my house could use some decorations for Christmas."

He regretted it the moment it left his mouth, but she disappeared with a grin. He was sure his house would be as outlandish as Myra was. She was the brightest and most colorful woman he knew. And she even changed the color of her hair and shoes to match whatever she had on her body. He was going to come home to a house in plaid, he knew it.

His grandma was waiting for him at the diner, and as he made his way there, he thought about what he was about to do, which was be publicly humiliated. His grandma would tell him that he was being silly — or worse, selfish — if he wasn't willing to give it a shot, but Sterl had taken a good hard look at his work and knew people were going to be disturbed by it.

He'd been hurt. Badly. Not just from the accident that had killed some of his friends, but the she-devil that had done it to them all. This thing, a true she-devil, had decided that, for whatever reason, he was going to father the monsters she was going to use to take over the world. She had invaded his dreams, his mind, as well as his health to get what she wanted. It had taken his family all working together with a pair of witches, Chris Bentley and Myra, as well as a demon, to set him free of her and get her out of his life. And painting had helped him do that.

He joined his grandma at the table and she laughed at him. Sterl loved his grandma, all of his family really, but this woman could make him feel like he was king of the world with just a smile. But today, he wasn't sure that he had it in him.

"I'm not really thrilled about this. First of all, they're going to laugh at us, and secondly, I'm not sure this is going to get me anywhere but in a loony bin." She told him he was going to be fine. "You keep saying that, and I'm not any closer to believing you than I was before you got this idea in your head."

"Darling, have I ever steered you wrong before?" He shook his head. "Then you just have to believe me that this is going to be good for you. You might even have to give me credit with your family over this. Especially your grandda. He's been an old poop lately."

9

"I'll give you credit either way. And Grandda is always a poop when he wants to be. He's never going to believe that he's wrong about anything." She slapped her hand gently on his. "When do we have to meet this person?"

"In two hours. I thought we'd leave now and then have plenty of time. You have your work in the car?" He assured her that he'd wrapped up what she'd told him to bring. "Good. You'll see, Sterling, this will be just perfect. Why, I'd bet by the end of this meeting, he'll be begging for more of your work. And I'd not be surprised if he wants to set things up right away. His family has been in this business for a very long time, and they know quality work when they see it."

He was driving them there slowly, even though the snow had stopped now, it was still slick. He hated to drive in this type of weather, or any for that matter, but they were going to get this over with. Then there was the fact that several times along the way he thought about pulling over and throwing up. This was a bad idea, and he wasn't sure that anyone would think his work was anything but crap. But he gripped his steering wheel and drove to what he was considering the last stand.

~~~

Isaac was excited to have his meeting. He knew that he was supposed to be doing a favor for a very nice person. Jasmine Calhoun had been a friend of his mother and grandmother for a very long time. And was now becoming one of his. He looked at his watch again and saw that the meeting was just over an hour away, and decided to go and find his brother.

Robert, even as his twin, was as different from him as they could get. While Isaac was tall and thin, Rob was five or so inches shorter and heavier. Not fat, not yet anyway, but not slim either. Laziness attributed to most of his weight gain, and drugs the rest of it. Isaac thought his divorce was making him drink more. Their mother had always thought it was Isaac's fault because he'd been successful and Rob hadn't. The logic of his mom had been out there, but he'd hired Rob to help when pressed by his parents just before they both were killed a few months ago in an accident.

Robert had been born second. And his birth, according to his parents, had just about ended his mom's life. Not true. Isaac had done some investigating and found that neither delivery had been that bad, and that their mom had sailed through both like a trooper. The only thing that had happened was their father, Robert also, had passed out when told there was a second child.

Robert, his brother, was sleeping on the floor behind his desk, naked, when Isaac went into his office. He'd been there when Isaac had left last night and covered him up with a blanket from his office. Shaking his head, he woke his brother with a kick to his feet. It was nearing one o'clock, and it looked as if he'd not moved since he left him on the floor last night at six.

"What the fuck, Isaac? Can't a person take a little breather without you waking them up? Go away and leave me alone. I have a pounding headache and you're not helping." He told him no, that when at work he expected him to do just that, work. "Well, I've gotten a lot done if you want to know the truth. I've been really busy until about ten minutes ago."

"Oh yeah? Well, then you're better than most. You've been there on the floor since last night. Might have been longer, but I went home and you were there. What the hell have you been doing if not sleeping?" Robert only glared at him as he sat up. There were two empty bottles under him, large ones of some sort of liquor. "Robert, I told you no drinking while here. You can do whatever you want at home, but no alcohol here at work. Damn it, this is a job, not a playroom for you to enjoy yourself in."

"You have no idea what I'm suffering with, Isaac. You should cut me some slack. Mary left me and took my children." He told him to get up and clean himself up. "I will. Christ, you're a hard ass. Why I ever thought working for you would be a piece of cake

11

I have no idea."

Isaac didn't say what was right on the tip of his tongue. He could have pointed out that if he'd been less of a drunk, or perhaps gotten a paying job instead of stealing, she might have stayed. Or that his children never saw him because he was either too drunk to move or at a bar. The fact that he was unhappy at not seeing them now was senseless. Then there was the added fact that the divorce had been finalized almost a year and a half ago, not recently as Robert tended to let people think.

"I have a meeting at two, so you need to get cleaned up and sober before they arrive. I want you to be in it with me so that you can see how it works." Robert said he didn't think he wanted to. "Rob, I gave you a job against my better judgement. And so far, you've done nothing toward making me think I've made even a reasonable investment. Either start working or I will fire you."

"Yeah? And what do you think Mom would say to that? You hired me because she told you to. You won't be able to fire me for the same reason. You owe me. I've not had as easy a life as you have. And my family left me. Mom is gone now, but you know as well as I that a death promise is the worst kind to break." He laid back down as he continued. "I'm going to take a nap then go to lunch. I don't even know if I'll return."

Isaac Sullivan wasn't a violent man. He rarely lost his temper even a little, but right now he thought he could have easily beaten the living shit out of Robert and not felt a single bit of regret. As he stood up, he snatched the blanket off his brother and smiled when he started cursing at him. Going to his own office, he sat at his desk and pulled up the camera that he had installed in Rob's office right before hiring him.

At the advice of his attorney, he'd done what he'd been told to keep his brother in line. It hadn't worked so far, and for whatever reason, Isaac was sure that it never would. The camera, Blake had told him, would go a long way in making sure that when he did end up firing Robert, not if but when, that he'd have enough evidence on him to make it stick. Just as he was ready to turn it off, he saw the rewind button and went back to noon yesterday. More than twenty-four hours before.

Rob was at his desk, but he wasn't alone. He had two women in the room with him, one of them naked on his desk, the other down on her knees in front of him. It was sickening to see Robert naked, but he watched as not only did the sex get violent, but one of the women had been hurt when Rob hit her hard enough to have her lying still nearly an hour later. Isaac thought he had to watch it then, if for no other reason than to make sure that Robert hadn't dragged the dead woman off somewhere and left her to rot.

He didn't watch his brother, but the woman. She wasn't moving, and it wasn't until Robert had finished that the other woman had gone to help her up. Both women staggered out of the room and into the elevator. He wondered why no one had commented on it, and was surprised to watch the guards turn their backs on the two as they left the building.

It took him nearly ten minutes to figure out what was going on. It wasn't that they were covering for Rob, but more than likely figured since he was his brother there would be nothing done about it. Isaac decided that he was going to have a little talk with his security team and end this shit once and for all. Going down in the elevator, he also decided to fire his brother today. To hell with his mom and the death promises she'd made him agree to. If Robert wasn't such an ass, he might have glossed over everything. But Robert was, and was going to cause them a great deal of trouble at the rate he was going.

After five minutes of talking with his team, Isaac knew that what he had guessed was correct. Nor was it the first time that his brother had done this. He'd been bringing in not just women, but all sorts of people during and after hours at his own pleasure.

13

After assuring the security team that they'd not lose their jobs, he asked if they had all the records of when he'd brought women in. It had occurred a total of seven times in the five weeks that Robert had been employed there. And that wasn't counting the night shift, which was supposed to do the same thing. Fuck.

"All right. This is what I want you to do. He's in his office. I'd like for you to go up there and help him leave." Bill, his top guard, just quirked a brow at him. "I don't care if you have to drag him out by his feet, I want him out of here now. And I'll call my attorney to tell him what I've done. Oh, you should take precautions when touching him. He's naked. Christ, why did I ever do this? Anyway, get him out of here now."

"He's not going to be happy. From what I've observed, he's pretty much made this place his play house." Isaac nodded and told him he was sorry. "No need for you to be sorry, sir. It's us that should be. He told us when he started here that you'd given him the keys to the place, and that if he didn't get his way, we'd be fired. We all have families, and this is a good job despite having to deal with him. I'm just sorry that we believed him."

"I didn't know. I want you to know that, I didn't know." Bill told him again that he should have told him from the start. "It's fine. We'll get him out of here and moved on. I don't think it'll be as easy as that, but I want him gone."

After talking to his attorney, he decided that he was going to be all right. That nothing could come back and bite him in the ass. However, the moment that the elevators opened, Isaac could hear his brother cursing, and the men helping him laughing.

"Isaac, I certainly hope you have a good reason for this. This is no way to treat your brother and your partner. Tell them to let me go." He said that he did have a good reason, and that they were not partners in anything. "Well, I can't imagine what it would be. And I told you that we should sign off on us being fifty-fifty in this place. Now I'm not so sure that I want to. Tell

14

these men to unhand me and I'll not call my attorney. You know as well as I do that this isn't going to look good in the papers. You're supposed to have this great reputation, right? How do you think this is going to look?"

"I do have one. But you do not. And I don't care for the way you've mistreated me and this gallery, so I think, in that regard, I can finally do something about it. You're fired, Rob. And it's no less than you deserve after all the things that you've done, not to mention not done since you've been here." Robert asked him if he was talking about the missing cash. "No. I was talking about the hookers that you brought in. What missing money?"

"What did you expect me to do? Live off what you were paying me? Fuck that shit. I sold a few of the paintings that were here, as well as got into the safe. It wasn't like you would miss anything. And I was right, you didn't." Robert laughed and jerked from the guard. "I'm willing to forget this whole thing if you just give me a little more each week, say about another grand, and I'll think about not calling the police or my attorney. You know I will, Isaac. I'm not kidding around this time. This is just stupid."

"I don't care. And you don't have an attorney, Robert. The one that I have, I pay. What will you do for money if you do find one to sue me? They require you to shell out some cash when you're asking them to do something for you." He looked at the men standing with Robert. "Take him out, please, and don't forget to get his badge as well as any company keys he has on him. Bill, will you please inform the parking garage that Robert no longer works here, and not to allow him to park on the premises? Thank you. And good luck, Robert. I have a feeling that you're going to need it."

He was handed the badge as well as Rob's parking permit and a key ring that had more keys on it than he'd given him. Such as one to the front door, as well as the conference rooms. When asked, Rob said he'd stolen his keys and made copies of them. Isaac asked him where he'd gotten them.

"I'm your brother. Surely you didn't think I should be begging to be let in and out of this place. For Christ's sake, Isaac, you should treat me better than you do." He asked him why. "I'm telling you right now, Isaac, if you do this, you're going to regret it for a very long time. I'm not one to fuck with. I have friends in very high places, you know."

"You're fired, Robert. And I'm not frightened of you. I'm also going to inform you that you'll have to find yourself transportation, as the limo service will no longer be there for you. Also, any and all paintings that you've taken from here and sold will have to be paid for, by you." Robert said he wasn't paying. "We'll see about that."

As he was taken out the door, three men dragging him across the floor, Isaac leaned back against the wall and tried to think why his brother was like this. He knew that it was his mom for the most part, but Dad hadn't helped either. When Bill told him it was done, he thanked him again.

"No need for that. But if you think this is done, then you'd be mistaken." Isaac said he was aware of that and wanted him to take precautions. "I can do that. I'll have some extra guards at the parking garage as well as in the lobby. Also, if you don't mind, I'll have the locks changed out. I have no doubt that he would have made more than one copy."

"You're more than likely right. Also, I'd like for you to detain anyone that comes here looking for Robert. I have a feeling that we've not heard the last of them either." Bill asked him if his brother really told on him like he was five. "Yes. And has done it our entire life, even when it wasn't possible for me to have done whatever misdeed he blamed on me. But promising my mom that I'd make sure that Robert had a job when I knew that I shouldn't was one of the biggest mistakes I've ever made."

Looking at his watch, he realized that his appointment was in twenty minutes. Isaac wasn't nearly as excited as he had been, but also, he was relieved that his brother wasn't going to be there to fuck things up. He'd known it was a mistake taking Robert on, but he thought that at thirty-seven, he might have grown up a bit.

The Calhouns arrived right on time. He liked Mrs. Calhoun anyway, and found that he truly enjoyed the company of the younger man. As he showed them around the gallery, he had only one thought in his head. This man was going to be famous if his work was half as good as his grandmother had told Isaac.

He pointed out places where he thought his work would be best displayed. Isaac also mentioned the preopening that he wanted to have, as well as the fliers to be printed, and who was catering the event. Sterling said nothing, but he could see the gleam of excitement in his eyes. The man was as shy about his work as Jasmine had told him.

"Now, you've seen the place. I'd very much like to see some of your work. When can we arrange it?" Sterling, Sterl he said to call him, told him that he had a few of his pieces in his car. Sending out the security team to bring them in, Isaac was impressed. "I have seen a few pictures of your work. Your grandmother was most accommodating. And if it's half as good as I think it'll be, you're going to have a wonderful gallery presence."

"Grandma told me that there was no point in waiting, that I should just show you from the start. And while I'm happy for the opportunity to do this, please don't feel obligated in taking it because you're friends with her." Isaac assured him that he wouldn't do that. "You most likely won't care for them. I started painting again at a low point in my life, and I think that my work shows it. It's very dark. A lot of it is nightmarish in the way I've painted it, and a great many people might be upset by it."

As soon as the first painting was uncovered, Isaac could see the pain. Almost feel it in his own heart. The paintings were dark,

17

haunting, and revealed a great deal about the artist. He hadn't had an easy time in his life, and he was good. Very good.

Isaac walked around the six paintings four times. Each time he looked at each of them, he saw a little more. Felt a little harder the pain of the man. There was a great deal of feeling in them, none of it good. But the work on them, the art, was outstanding. More than that, it was perfection. As he stood in front of the last one again, he asked Sterl if he had any more.

"Yes. Ten more. All with the same darkness. I'm not there any longer, but I still feel the need to put it to canvas. I don't know that I'll ever feel a need to paint landscapes." Isaac told him that he hoped he never painted those. "You don't care for them, do you? It's all right. I understand that—"

"Sterl, I think you're amazing. I'd like to run a gallery opening with all your work." Sterl was shaking his head. "I'm serious. These are...words fail me on how good these are. And the darkness of them will appeal to a great many people on all kinds of levels. Yes, we're going to do well, you and I."

CHAPTER 2

Marty hated the woman that she was training. Well, maybe not hate, but she really disliked her. There was something so... she wasn't sure what it was about her that just set her anger off, but it could have been any number of things. The way that she kept referring to her as Mabel, Mary, or any other name other than her own. Or it might have been the way she kept fussing with her makeup and clothing that made her want to spill water down the front of her, but what truly irritated her the most was how she kept referring to herself in the third person. "Bethany is going to be so good at this job." Or her favorite so far was, "Bethany doesn't need this job, but Daddy said that she must work to earn her keep."

Waitressing wasn't a job for the meek, Marty thought. And she would bet that Bethany would tell herself after the first few hours on her own that Bethany didn't need to earn her keep that badly. As they were headed to the table to take an order, she heard her telling herself that she must get some nicer pens. She'd soon learn that was a total waste of money.

"Howdy. Can I get you guys anything to drink before you order?" The man nodded and smiled at her. The woman was looking over the menu. "We have iced tea and pop. Coffee if you've a mind, too."

"My wife would like a large iced tea, no lemon or sugar, and I'd like a glass of water. No lemon for me either."

Just as Marty was walking away, Bethany started talking to them. "Bethany thinks that you should drink lemon in your water. I'll make sure that you have plenty of it. No water should ever be without some sort of citrus taste it in." She smiled at the big man and then looked at her. "He wants lemon at Bethany's recommendation."

"No, he doesn't. Do you?" The man shook his head no. "See? No lemon. In either drink. Now, we'll go and get them—"

"Bethany thinks it would taste better. You should listen to me. That's the way I like it." Marty just walked away to get the drinks, and when she was putting ice in the glass to take to the couple, Bethany huffed at her. "Men are just so stubborn. Why do they not listen to Bethany when she's correct in this? At least put some lemons on a plate for them. He'll thank you for it."

"No, he will not. He said, twice now, that he doesn't want lemons. Don't try and add things to people's orders when they specifically said no to them. Not only will you tick them off, but you're going to make it so that they don't tip you. And I don't know if anyone told you this or not, but tips are what we strive for in this business." Bethany started to fuss about how she liked lemons and the man just didn't know what he was missing. "I'm sure that he's a grown man and knows what a lemon tastes like in water. Don't do it."

Marty had to back away from Bethany when she started to put a handful of lemons in the glass of water. Just as she was trying to scoot around her, her boss came out of the back room. Bethany told him that Marty was messing up the order.

"Are you?" Marty told Wilmer what had been said and what Bethany wanted her to do. He looked over at the other woman. "We don't add to people's drinks or orders, Bethany, unless they want it. It doesn't sound as if he wanted it."

"That's because he's dumb when it comes to knowing what is good for him. Bethany drinks water all the time with lemon in it, and it's the only way to drink it. If Margie would just listen, he'd thank her for it."

Marty left them there and headed for the table. The man was laughing when she handed him his glass of water. It was a nice sound, hearty and strong. The woman was laughing as well, and she smiled at them both. Then she asked them if they were ready to order.

"Yes. Thanks." She wrote down their order. She wasn't surprised by the fact that the man wanted three burgers and only a single order of fries. He was a big man. The woman wanted onion rings instead of the fries with her burger, and didn't care that it was going to be fifty cents more. "Also, could you bring us some of the pie now? My wife has been wanting rhubarb pie for a week now."

"Of course. Ice cream too?" The woman moaned and Marty smiled. It was good pie and she liked it herself. "I'll bring it right out. Oh, and I'm training the other woman. Please let me know if you have any problems."

"She's never going to make it."

Marty thought he was correct but said nothing. She didn't understand why Bethany thought she could make it work.

The woman had been on the job since seven-thirty. She'd been told to be there at five-thirty, but Bethany didn't like coming in that early so they'd have to make sure that they didn't start until then. Maybe she thought breakfast was an afternoon meal, but Wilmer had only told her to be on time tomorrow.

Marty went to put their order in just as Bethany was told, again, to listen to her if she wanted to be any good at her job. Wilmer told Marty he was sorry for this, but as she was the best, there was no hope for anyone else trying to train Bethany. If it could even be done. Marty told him she was fine, so long as

Bethany didn't try to sabotage her customers.

Just as she was cutting a large piece of the pie for the woman, Bethany came to stand near her again and started asking questions. And as usual she had a reason for why things should be done her way.

"You gonna eat that while you're working?" She told her no, that it was for the couple. "Bethany doesn't think that's right. Dessert before eating your meal? Let me have it and I'll make sure they get it when they're done."

"No. Damn it, Bethany. They want it now and I'm going to take it to them. Just watch and learn. These people, or any of the customers, do not need for you to make comments or judgments on what they're doing." Bethany huffed at her and told her she was doing it all wrong. "Whatever."

She'd had enough, and was almost willing to let her finish waiting on these people so she could fuck it up. But Marty liked her job a great deal, and didn't want to give poor service to anyone. As she took the pie to the table again with a large scoop of ice cream on it, Marty prayed that Bethany would keep her mouth shut. No such luck.

"She insisted on bringing you this now, and Bethany is going to take it back." The woman said nothing, but looked at her when the pie was placed on the table. Just as Bethany reached for it, the woman slapped her hand down on Bethany's. "You can have it later, but not before your meal. Bethany thinks that you'll enjoy it better if you—"

"Bethany, is it?" She nodded at the woman. "Bethany, if you try and take my pie I will get up and kick your ass all over this room. Now, back away before one of us gets hurt. I asked for it now and I'm going to enjoy it now. Go back to the kitchen and mind your own business."

"I don't think you understand what Bethany is trying to do for you. You can't have your dessert first. It's not the way that things go." Bethany reached for the plate again, and the low growl coming from the woman had Marty backing up. She knew the sound all too well because she knew quite a few shifters. "You're being very rude right now, and Bethany just doesn't appreciate it. I'm taking this pie."

Marty put her fingers in her mouth and blew out a shrill sound. Not only did the entire restaurant quiet down, but Wilmer came out to see what had happened. The big man stood up and the woman stayed where she was, enjoying her pie. Mr. Calhoun, as the man said was his name, told Wilmer what had happened.

"My wife and I came in to have an enjoyable lunch, and we were going to have pie. You see, my wife wanted some because it brought her fond memories. The first waitress, Marty, did a great job, but then this other woman just came barging in, telling us what was going to happen and how we were going to do things her way. I don't think you're going to stay in business long if you keep hiring people like her." Marty was surprised by the man's tone as well as his words. It was soft yet firm, like his word was the only one, and he was telling it in such a way she thought he was used to having people listen to his every word and taking it as gospel. "I'm not telling you what to do, sir, but I'd think about how she's made us feel, and we've only been here for a few minutes. I can't imagine that she'd make anyone coming in for an entire meal feel any better than we do about her service."

"I'm so very sorry, Mr. Calhoun. I'll get on your order right away, and it's on us today." Mr. Calhoun said that wasn't necessary. "But it is. As I said, I'm very sorry for this misunderstanding, and I'll take care that it's made right."

Marty waited on the couple, even had a good time talking to them about nothing at all. And as Bethany was nowhere to be seen, she also got to take them what they ordered without any judgment from the other woman.

When they were finished, she was glad for the large tip that they left her despite them not paying for their meal. Walking away with the hundred dollars, Marty knew she was going to be able to pay her rent and have money left over for a movie on her birthday in two days. Going to night school was taking all her extra time and cash right now.

Bethany was gone by the time she was ready to finish her shift, going home because she had things to do. Marty worked both breakfast and lunch for the tips so didn't miss her at all. Wilmer was standing by the clock when she went to punch out. He asked if he could talk to her. When they were in the office, she noticed that he wasn't his usual happy self and asked him what was wrong.

"Mr. Dolan wants me to fire you." Marty sat back in her chair and asked why the owner would want that. "I had no idea, but Bethany Flynn is his girlfriend. She came in here telling me that her daddy wanted her to have a job, but it wasn't her daddy but her sugar daddy. He's pissed that I had the nerve to fire her after she'd done such a good job. I'm guessing her version of what happened today is much different than what really happened."

"I would certainly think so. Damn it all to hell and back, Wilmer. What am I going to do now? Does he have any idea how fucked up that is?" He nodded, then shook his head. "I'm assuming that you told him how things went down today, didn't you?"

"Yes, but as I said, my version and hers differ too much for him to believe me. She must have told him a whopper of a story. I'm so sorry, Marty. I wouldn't have hired her at all had.... Well, I might have because he would have made sure. But this is wrong, so wrong."

Nodding, she sat there. What was she going to do now? Where would she work that would allow her to go to school at night and make money daily to pay for food and rent? As she sat there, thinking about what she had just lost, Wilmer came around to the other side of his desk and sat in the chair next to her. He asked her if she was going to be all right.

"I don't think so." He nodded and handed her an envelope, telling her that it was two weeks of pay and a little more. "You know that you can't do this. He'll fire you next."

"I don't care. If I have to hire Bethany again, I'm going to quit anyway. You're the only reason that a great many of our regulars come in here. Without you, I don't think we're going to last that long." Marty took the envelope and stood up. "You go on home and try not to think about what has happened. Maybe in a couple of days, when a few more people are pissed off about her, he'll see reason."

For some reason, she didn't think she'd be so lucky. Not to mention, she wasn't sure that she wanted to work for a man that didn't care to find out facts before making such a call. Marty gathered her coat and things, cleaning out her locker while she was at it, and headed for the back door. Tyler, the cook, stopped her and handed her a large take out bag.

"You go on now and take it. Wilmer said you'd be skipping meals to pay your bills. Besides, they'll not miss a thing." She nodded and took the bag, as well as a sandwich that she'd planned to take home tonight. "That girl, I heard she was coming to work here for good. Can't think that's going to go over very well. She's a few slices short of a full loaf if you ask me. Where do them kinda girls come from, I ask you?"

"She's the boss's girlfriend, so I'd watch myself." He just shook his head. "Thank you for this, Tyler. Just don't get yourself in trouble over it."

"I won't. Like I said, they won't miss it a bit. And Wilmer, he helped me pack things in it. Not much, honey, but it'll keep you going for a bit." He hugged her and she left in tears. "I'll be calling you. You take care now, child."

Marty cried all the way home. She'd just gotten the biggest

tip of her life and lost her job in one hour. What the fuck was she going to do now? she wondered.

~~~

Trent was sitting in his office not really doing much of anything when his grandda came in. He had been in and out of the house for the last couple of days, asking questions about this and that. Trent asked him what he was up to now and he laughed.

"I was gonna ask you the same thing. Got a call today, not an hour ago, from a man by the name of Wilmer Mackey. Know him?" Trent said that the name sounded familiar, but no, he didn't know who he was. "I think you might remember him after I tell you about what he said. You and Joe had a nice meal at his diner yesterday. Just out of town."

"Oh yes. I remember him. Why is he calling you?" Grandda told him that he thought he was calling him. "I don't understand. Why was he calling anyone? He picked up our tab and that was the end of it. Is that Bethany person saying I did something to her?"

"Bethany Flynn." Trent nodded. "She is the girlfriend of the man who owns the place. You know him too. Roger Dolan. There was another waitress, you remember what her name was?"

"Yes, Marty. What's going on, Grandda? Did something happen that I should be aware of?" Grandda nodded and Trent noticed that he was upset about something. "What happened?"

"He fired her." Trent said good. "Not the bimbo—his words, not mine—but the waitress. Apparently, he had to do it because this Bethany person got her underwear all tightened up and wanted her gone. So, Dolan had Wilmer fire her."

"Why would he call you to tell you that?" Grandda got up and went to the window. "What are you not telling me about this? I have a feeling that you want to do something about it. Or to Dolan. Tell me so I can talk you out of it."

"What a way to talk to your own flesh and blood." He didn't

come back to sit and Trent was worried. There was more going on than he understood right now. "Her grandmomma, Sofie Hamilton, was a friend of mine and your grandma's. I knew her a long time ago, before you boys started coming along. Sophie raised Marty like her own daughter when her momma ran out on her. Then a few months ago, I heard that Sofie was gone and left her granddaughter with more bills than money."

"I'm sorry to hear that." Grandda nodded. "Have you been watching over them all this time? Sending them money and such?"

"In a way. I honestly never thought of them in the last few years. Oh, I'd have a thought to check up on them, but something else would come along and I'd be off again. But I did call in a few favors when I found out that she'd passed on to have her funeral paid up. I also had an attorney go by and talk to Marty, but she said she was doing just fine and didn't need any handouts. Going to college to become something more, she told him." Grandda wiped at his face with his white handkerchief and continued talking. "Wilmer, like I said, he was calling you when he got me. I think he just messed up the names is all. Anyway, he was calling you to see if you and I were related. Like I said, her grandmomma was a good friend of ours."

"So, he has to fire Marty and calls you to tell you. Does he want us to hire her? I mean, I can if that will help you out. We could always use a few hands around the clinic and such. Even helping out around here if you want." He shook his head. "Grandda, I want to help her too."

"I'm going to go and see her in the morning. I would have gone out there today, but she's not answering her phone. I guess she took it kind of hard, like I would have, to have lost her job to a woman like this Bethany person is." Trent told him what had happened at the restaurant. "Yeah, Wilmer told me about the same thing. Can you imagine talking about yourself like that? I'd

27

have to hit her. Anyway, I'd like for you to go with me. Or one of you guys. I might need some help convincing her that I'm not out to hurt her."

"I'll go." Then he remembered an appointment with Joe at the new plant and told him about it. "Take Elijah or Scott. They're not doing much this afternoon, and you can call and ask them. Or Sterl. I think he's supposed to be back with Grandma tonight."

"She said she would be. They got that thing going on." Trent started to ask what they were doing but his grandda spoke first. "Don't know, if that was what you were going to ask me. She's been plotting and planning and I tend to stay out of that when I can. Your grandma can find me work faster than anyone can when she thinks I'm being idle and all. Also, she's a little on the intense side when she's in that mood."

He knew that for a fact. "This woman, Marty, she's good at what she does waiting tables. You said she was going to college… you know what for?" Grandda said he didn't. "Well, whatever it is, perhaps we can help her out with that as well. We have that fund set up for the pack. I don't see any reason for us not to help out a friend too."

"That'd be nice of you, Trent. I worry about her. I don't know her that well. Only met her the one time, and she was a child then. Pretty little thing." Trent told him she'd grown into a beautiful woman too. "Her grandmomma, she was a pistol and a beauty too. Like a bear with claws when it came to something she'd set her teeth into. And that girl, I'm betting she's no different."

"I'd say that she isn't. Joe liked her as well." Grandda nodded but still looked upset. He told him that he was going to go and talk to one of the boys, his brothers, and he'd talk to him when he returned. "Let me know if you don't find someone. I can reschedule with Joe and I'll go with you."

Trent worked then. He'd been putting things off long enough and needed to make some more calls on businesses. He had to smile when he thought of Doug Coulier, the owner of the plastics manufacturing plant, and his romance. Anastasia, a very powerful fae, and he had been out of touch for the last week and a half. Being mates was exhausting those first few months, which made him think of his own wife.

Joe. He loved her with every fiber of his being. She was smart, powerful as well, and the best thing that had ever happened to him. They were set to go to the cabin this weekend, and he was getting excited about that. It was one of the reasons he was so far behind today, thinking of the fun they were going to have while there. He might even go ice fishing if the pond was frozen enough.

There were three e-mails from different manufacturing plants. Doug had told him a week ago that he'd refer a few of the people he knew wanted to relocate to him. Trent had been inundated with not just e-mails, but calls as well. If things worked out the way they appeared to be, they'd have every person who wanted a job working by the end of next year. They were already showing signs of better times with the two new shops opening, as well as a larger department store wanting to come in and the grocery store enlarging.

Things were looking up. More than he could have imagined several months ago when he'd taken over the pack. There were times when he wished that someone else was doing it. It was time consuming as well as stressful with the mess that had been left to him when he'd had to kill the previous alpha. Casey O'Neil had been ready to kill his mate, and Trent had leapt to her defense.

Joe came into his office just as he was finishing an e-mail and sending it off. She sat down in the big chair across from him and looked upset. He asked her if things were going all right on her end.

"Yes, I suppose. Did you know that there is only one doctor in this pack? The way we're growing...oh, before I forget, two

29

families will be calling you today to interview for the pack. But we have only the one doctor. That's too much for one person." He agreed and asked her what she'd done about it. "You're so positive that I did something?"

"Yes. You're the type that sees a problem and fixes it. It's not like you don't know that I'd okay whatever you wanted to do." She nodded. "How did you fix it?"

"I called in a few favors, and we now have a total of four health professionals coming to see if they'd like to take some of the load off Todd. He's excited that someone will be helping. And so you know, one of the buildings in the downtown area is being reequipped for a hospital of sorts. For now, just as an emergency room. Mostly for pack, but for anyone."

"Good idea. And these other doctors, when they get here, are we going to have any say in it, or have you assigned someone to take care that they have what they need?" She asked him what he meant. "I'm assuming that they've all specialized in things. Will someone be getting them housing? Equipment? Meds? Or will you be doing that as well?"

"Oh. That is going to be your brother, Tanner. He said that he has a couple of friends on some hospital boards that will guide him on contracts and such. And Noah is going to help as well. I'm not sure in what capacity at this point, but he said that he's on a few boards as well and will help out." Trent figured it was in good hands if they were going to be working on it. "I have set up a fund too, so that the pack doesn't have to pay out for everything. It won't be much, but I think it will be a good way for the community to get involved. Also, I've an appointment to speak to Doug about some investing when he comes up for air."

"Have you spoken to Anastasia?" She said that she hadn't but wasn't worried about her. "Me either. It's Doug that I worry about a little. Having a mate is the best, but it's also draining. And I would imagine more so with one of them being a fae."

"She's going to change him, I'm thinking. And with her age, there are some things that she can do that would keep them both safe. Noah can go out in daylight as well, but she can practically live out in the sun now." Trent nodded and looked at his computer when it sounded. "I'll let you get to work. I just wanted to let you know what I've been able to figure out."

Trent read over the e-mail three times before he got up and danced around the room laughing. It was from Sterl. Picking up his phone, he called his brother to congratulate him on his success.

CHAPTER 3

Marty had three interviews today. It was difficult to get around today since there was snow on every street, and the sidewalks weren't any better. Ohio weather was the dumbest thing. Today it was going to only reach a high of twenty-two. Then in two days it was supposed to get up to fifty-three.

She was just putting her phone back on the charger when someone knocked at her door. If it was the landlord again, she was going to hit him with her bat.

She opened the door with the bat in her hand. Marty, ready to tell him once again that she didn't need to move in with him to save rent, saw an elderly man with a taller younger one.

"You gonna hit us with that?" She put the bat back by the door and said she wasn't. "Glad to hear that. I'm James Calhoun. This is my grandson, Sterling. I was a friend of your grandmomma's."

"Yes. I remember her talking about you. And I think I waited on someone from your family the other day. His name was...I think it was Trent. Anyway, I'm sorry but I have to tell you that Grandma is gone now." He told her he knew. "I'm sorry. Won't you come in? I've been.... Come in."

Sterling stood there for several seconds, staring at her hard, like he found her lacking or something. She was ready to slam the door in his face and leave him out there, but Mr. Calhoun pulled him into the apartment. Marty saw her landlord coming up the stairs just as she was closing the door.

"You entertaining those men?" She said nothing, trying to think why he thought it was any of his business. "You won't live with me and put out for rent, but you're willing to take on strangers."

"I'm not even going to justify that with a comment. I'm not telling you again that I will pay my rent when it comes due." He crossed his arms over his chest and glared. Marty felt the man behind her but didn't turn. "Mr. Billows, I think it's time you went home to your wife. I'm sure she could use your help with those three kids of yours."

"I don't want you doing this. I already told you that we could work out a deal, you and me, that would benefit us both." The low growl from Sterling had her turning to look at him as Mr. Billows continued. "She's a pretty woman who is out of work. And I'm laying claim to her. You get on out of here before I call the police."

"You might want to call a coroner while you're at it. If you talk to her like that again, I'm going to tear your throat out." Mr. Billows looked like he was going to argue when Sterling moved to stand in front of her. "You had best be on your way before you bite off more than you can chew. And if you don't, I'm not going to hold back on how I treat a man who is abusive to women."

When he left, Marty turned to Sterling. He had this look about him, like he was on edge. Then she realized that the growls were telling her something that she'd only just realized. He was a shifter too. Turning to go back into her apartment, trying her best not to think about what he was, she looked at Mr. Calhoun.

"You're not human." He told her they were wolves. "I see. And the reason that you've come here? I'm assuming it has nothing to do with me but your friendship with my grandma. If that's so, then I will tell you that things are settled with her and her estate, and I'd like for you both to leave."

"Sterl?" The younger man looked at his grandfather and nodded. "Holy jumping beans. Never would have thought it would be now. Come on in, Sterl, Marty. We got some talking to do, and I think dinner out would be a bit more private than here."

"Talking about what?" Neither of them spoke and she looked at Sterling. "What is he talking about, and why are you acting like I've just hurt you in some way?"

"You know what we are." She nodded and said shifter, even though it wasn't a question. "Okay, well, I'm not sure how to tell you this but straight out. You're my mate."

"No." She moved to the kitchen area to make her a cup of tea. She wasn't sure why it calmed her, but the task of brewing a cup of tea made her think of her grandma and her being so focused on the task. Sterling came to stand near the sink as she worked. "Would you like a cup of tea before you guys leave? I'm a little short on flavors right now, but I do have some really good dark tea. I don't care for the flavored ones like Grandma did, but I can make you a cup. Again, before you both leave."

"May I talk to you about this?" She shook her head and pulled out two more of her favorite cups and saucers. "Grandda doesn't drink tea, but I will have a cup. But I'd very much like to talk to you about this."

"There's nothing to talk about. As I said before, I'm doing just fine on my own, and I don't want to be rude, but I have no desire to be a mate to anyone. Not even engaged to anyone. I like my life, by myself, just the way it is." He said nothing, and she wasn't sure that she wanted him to. Marty had been around mates enough to know that they were a weird group of people. "I have things to do today, so if you and your grandfather would say whatever it is you need to and go, I'd be happy."

"Let me start by telling you a bit about myself. I'm an artist. Yesterday my grandma took me to see this gallery owner, and

35

he wants to put my paintings in his place to sell. I was thinking that I'd put like fifty bucks on them and hope that they'd sell, but he put tens of thousands of dollars on them and he's already sold one. I don't know why I'm telling you this other than I needed to say it aloud for me. I'm a wolf, a pureblood. I think you understand and know what a shifter is." She nodded and watched him. "I have no idea what to say to you about not being my mate. It's a done deal, so I don't know what to do from here. I never, especially in the last few years, thought that I'd find my other half, and here you are. I've had a rough time of it of late."

"You're babbling, and I have a feeling that it's not a normal thing with you. But I'm sorry to hear about your rough times. I've not had such a good time either of late. And congratulations on your art. I have no hidden talent like that, other than I'm good with people. I lost my job recently." He said that Trent was his brother. "I see, so you know the whole sordid tale."

"Yes. Trent is very sorry that you were fired. I guess he feels like Joe does, that you were shafted by the owner. Do you know him well?" Marty handed him his cup of tea and said she'd only spoken to him when he'd pop into the restaurant. "He's an ass. Tanner, one of my other brothers, knows him well. I guess he has a wife and a couple of kids in addition to this other woman."

"We have to talk, you two. I mean, you can't stay here if that guy thinks you're gonna be his play thing." She told Mr. Calhoun that she wasn't worried about Mr. Billows. "Well, you might want to now. With Sterl being your mate and all, he ain't gonna be long for this world if he pulls that crap on you again."

Marty looked at Sterling. "Is he right? You'd hurt him for thinking that he can try and get me to sleep with him?" Sterling shook his head. "Well, that's good news. I don't think it would be all that nice to hurt—"

"I'd not hurt him, but kill him." She felt her fear of the man wash over her. "I'd never harm you. Not that I could, but I wouldn't anyway. But if he thinks he can bully you into something like this, then he needs to be taught a lesson."

"By killing him." Sterling said if it was necessary. "Killing someone is never necessary. He has a wife and children. What are they supposed to do if you kill him for no other reason than he wants to get into my pants?"

He growled and she slapped him. It was that or run in fear from him, and Marty had had enough running. She was taking a stand against people who thought they'd run her life. When his nose started to bleed, she handed him a towel and bit her lower lip so she'd not tell him she was sorry. She was, but he didn't have to know that.

Mr. Calhoun laughed. It started out low, just a hiccup of one, but now he was holding onto the couch laughing hard enough that she was sure he was going to hurt something. And when she asked him what was so funny, he laughed all the harder. These men were very strange.

"I think it's time that you both left. I'm not sure why you even came here in the first place, but I have things to do today." Sterling leaned against the counter. "Or I can just go. As I said, I have things to do."

"Finding a job won't be necessary. I talked to Wilmer yesterday. He told me that he feels really bad about you losing your job like you did. He said that he gave you a few bucks, but it'd not be enough to keep you in bread and butter for long." She looked at Sterling as Mr. Calhoun sat there talking. He was sipping his tea like he was set to stay with her until hell froze over. "Also, you might want to have some say in things going on at Sterl's house. He's been working on it since I've come back to town."

"I'd not have to work on it still if you were to stay away from the contractors. You keep changing things up with them and they have to find me to okay them. And now that Alta is involved,

I might not have too much in the way of home sweet home when we get back. Did you see how Myra decorated it? Christ, Grandda, it's beautiful, but over the top. Why did you think I needed a bigger kitchen and dining room anyway?" They both looked at her. "Okay, I guess that makes sense. But you didn't know about her before this."

"No, but a man can hope, can't he? And with your brother having twins soon, and then there is Joe and Chloe around too, mayhap we can be bouncing a lot of them on our knees." He looked over at her. "You like kids? I do. Lots of them."

"They're all right, I guess. I never really thought about it. But if this is your sly way of getting me to say I want them, it won't work. I don't want to have any kind of relationship with Sterling here anymore than I think he does with me. You two need to go home now." Neither one moved. "Seriously, you two are overstaying your welcome."

Mr. Calhoun stood up and she felt herself relax a little. With them gone she'd be able to think. Right now, all she could think about was what this man would demand of her should she agree to this harebrained idea of being his mate. No way, no how. But when she looked at Sterling, she saw that he wasn't budging and she wanted to stomp her foot at him.

When the elderly Calhoun left them, laughing as he did so, she asked Sterling when he was going. Instead of answering her, he moved to her couch and sat down. Saying nothing, she made her way to her bedroom and locked the door. She needed to get ready for her interviews, and whatever he wanted to do while she was out was up to him.

It took her nearly an hour to get ready. It wasn't something normal for her, to primp and play with her hair and makeup, but the man in her living room was distracting her. And for some reason she wanted to look pretty. Marty kept telling herself that it wasn't for him, but every time she glanced in the mirror at herself, she did wonder, only a little, what he'd think about her appearance. Finally, she gathered her coat and purse and headed to the living room. Sterling was waiting by the door for her.

~~~

Sterl helped her on with her coat, against her wishes of course, but he was enjoying himself. As they made their way out of the apartment building, he put his arm around her and pulled her a little closer when the landlord came out of his door. He'd have to be dealt with, and soon. Marty refused to get into his car when they were standing in front of it.

"I can walk." He said that he was aware of that, but that he didn't want her to. "You want a lot of things, don't you? Well, I have interviews all over town, and I won't have you sitting out in the car waiting on me. Your grandfather won't care for it either."

"He won't care. In fact, I bet when you're between interviews, he'll talk your arm off. If my dad was here, he would. My dad is a talker." She glared at him and did the most incredible thing... she stomped her foot at him. "You're adorable. I can't believe my luck in finding you today."

"You didn't find me because I wasn't lost. I was right here, all by myself, having a life. I don't need, nor do I want, you in it." He smiled at her. "I don't even like you."

"I can live with that. We've only just met. But if you were to get hurt falling on the ice or were too cold, I'd never forgive myself. You're my mate." She growled at him and he laughed. "I've not had much of a reason to laugh lately, so I thank you for that."

"You're odd." Sterl told her that he'd been called a lot worse. "What is this tragic thing that has changed you into a sour man? I can only assume it was tragic, because you're otherwise seemingly nice and normal."

"A she-devil thought that I'd make a nice alpha to her, and decided to kill all the people I was with one night and poison me

39

with her magic. She decided that I'd be perfect in helping her create an army of monsters like her. And not only did she not stop there, but she also put into my memories and thoughts the need to kill anyone who tried to help me. I wanted to die, mostly every minute of every day. But this vampire friend of mine and his day walker helped by calling in a witch. It saved my life, because I was ready to throw in the towel and end it all. I would have, too, had it not been for the fact that I'm an immortal. You too, now that I've found you." He kissed her on the mouth when she stood staring at him. "You're looking like you don't believe me."

"A she-devil? A witch and a vampire? How stupid do I look to you?" Sterl asked her if she didn't believe in them. "I do, at least the vampire and witch, but a she-devil? No, not so much. And what do you mean, an army of monsters?"

"She thought I was an alpha, do you know what that is?" She nodded at him and he wanted to kiss her again, but decided that perhaps if he explained things to her better, she'd be more inclined to allow it. Not to mention, she'd not hit him again. "Okay, she thought that since I was an alpha, which I guess I could be, my seed would be stronger for it. And she was thrilled that I was a wolf. Her thinking was that her monsters would be stronger for it, and being able to shift would help them kill. The plan in her head was that should she get her little monsters from me, they'd be able to take over the world and I'd be with her for all time. I have no idea why she thought that I'd just agree to such a plan, but that's what happened. That is until I was able to draw first blood and injure her before she could kill me."

When she shivered, he took off his coat and put it around her. She didn't object, but he thought it was due more to her thinking about what he'd said than letting him protect her from the cold. As they stood there, he gently wrapped his arm around her and guided her to the car. It really was too cold for her to be out in it. Once he had her in the truck, Sterl wasn't thinking that he'd won any round with her, but was sure there were going to be fireworks when she realized it. He asked her where her first interview was.

"Berry's Steakhouse just out of town." It was out of town and about ten miles from where she lived. Sterl asked if she had a car. "No. It was on its last legs when Grandma was alive, but once she was gone, there wasn't enough money for gas anyway. Where is this she-devil now?"

"She's.... Her maker came to get her." Marty asked him what that meant. "I'm trying to give you this a little at a time. I don't want to overwhelm you. But a demon named Richard came and got her because we drew first blood. It was part of the pact he'd made with her when she'd been created. A long time ago, as a matter of fact. Richard took her to his lair and made her his sexual slave. Her parents too, I heard."

Marty was quiet for the rest of the ride. The roads were bad so he had to concentrate on keeping the car on the road and not in a ditch all the way there. Grandda talked to them both quietly too, but Marty didn't say anything back to him. When they pulled up in front of the restaurant, she looked out the front of the car.

"I'm late. I'm thinking that this is not going to bode well for me and a job." Sterl wanted to tell her that she didn't need to work when he realized perhaps she did. Not for the money—he had plenty—but for her own self-worth. "Will you be here when I get back? The reason I'm asking is, I think I might have overestimated my ability to get around in this stuff without help."

"We'll be right here waiting for you." Marty nodded but didn't move out of the truck. "We could just go back to your place if you'd rather."

"I don't know what to do. I don't.... This is all so very strange to me. While no she-devil tried to take me, I've had a shitty couple of days. And my birthday is tomorrow. I just wanted to have a nice few days off and then go back to work on Sunday to make

41

up the money in tips." Sterl said nothing, not even sure what to say. "I'm out of work. I have about two hundred dollars to my name after I paid my rent for the month, and I don't know what I'm going to do now. I'm not sure how I'll react when he tells me that he won't hire me."

When she started to cry, he pulled over into a parking space and held her to him. The sobs were tearing at his heart, but he didn't comment. He knew from watching his brothers that there were times when it was better if you didn't say a word but let them ramble. Not that she was saying anything either, but he held her all the same. Grandda got out of the car and made his way into the restaurant.

"He didn't have to leave. I'm okay now." Sterl let her go when she pulled away. "I've been under a lot of stress the last few days, that's all. I'm not usually so weepy."

"I can tell that." She looked up at him and he wiped at a tear that was on her cheek. "I have an idea. I'm sure you're not going to like it, but I'd like to propose that we go back to your place, pack a few things up, and you come out to the house with me. I will let you have your pick of rooms and you can spend a few days getting to know us all. And let me tell you, it's a lot to take in with this family. That way we can have a wonderful birthday dinner, just the two of us. Celebrate it any way you want, and then you can get some much needed rest."

"Why are you doing this? And don't tell me it's because you have some sort of idea that this will change my mind. It won't. I don't need any more stress in my life." He said he just wanted her to relax for a few days. "It's more than that, isn't it?"

"Some, but nothing you need to be worried over. I do want you to relax. I also want you to meet my family. They're a big lot, too noisy most of the time, but they're as kind and generous as they can be. And I love them with all my heart." She looked at the restaurant. "I would like for you to come home with me."

"This doesn't mean that I'm agreeing to anything." He said he understood that. "I just...I have no idea why I think this is a good idea other than I'm nuts, but I'll do it. Under a few conditions. No sex. I don't know you well enough for that, and I might never know you that well. Also, when I want to go, you take me back. Or have your brother do it."

He nearly told her that they'd not live if they tried, but nodded. She'd understand that soon enough. Calling out to his grandda, he told him the plan. Grandda said he'd be out in a moment, he had something to check on.

When he finally got in the car, he was angry but didn't say about what. Sterl thought that whatever had happened in there, he'd tell him about it later. But he told him before he could speak again.

She's all worked up. I hate that. To have someone so sweet and innocent just upset like this. I'm not mad, mind, but just upset. He told grandda that he was as well. *You make her happy, Sterl. She needs it.* Sterl agreed, then told Marty what had happened yesterday at the gallery.

"I took in four pieces of my work. This guy, Isaac Sullivan, was really excited about them, and once he looked them over, he was talking contracts and showings. Like it was a done deal." He drove slowly, but was enjoying it because she was coming to his house. "He asked me how many more I had at home and I told him ten, but I really have a bit more. Not all of them were as dark as the ones that I brought him, but nearly so. He said that he thought they'd all sell before the showing. I was okay with that. I mean, I was going to use the money to buy more canvases and paint. Never did I dream that he'd be putting such high tags on them."

"I've been to the Sullivan Gallery. They do a great job putting things in all price ranges. And they have a little gift shop where I've gotten a couple of things for Grandma in over the years.

43

You're very lucky to have gotten in with them. They've been around for a little while, but made a great name for themselves." Sterl told her that he was glad his grandma had found them as well. "What sort of dark work do you do?"

"The she-devil…I told you that she was in my memories. I painted that night that she killed my friends from memory. And some of the nightmares that I had because of what she'd done to me." Marty nodded and Grandda asked about the showing. "It's in November. I have to gather up four more pieces that I want to sell, and then let him have the others for showing. Not to sell, you see. Which I don't know why he thinks they'll sell at all, but he called me before I came here to tell me that he had a buyer on one of them. For twelve thousand dollars."

"Wow, lucky you. And I'd love to see them. I don't know a lot about art, but I do like it. To see someone's work that they spent so much of themselves creating is a wonderful sight. If you don't mind, that is." He smiled and told her it would be his pleasure. "Great. Maybe you'll sell them all and be able to buy yourself a lot of paint and canvas."

Sterl thought with the sale of the first painting that he'd be able to do that. Especially since most of what he'd picked up was from auctions and garage sales. Yes, he was going to be able to afford a lot more in the way of supplies now.

Chapter 4

The house, much too tame of a word for this place, was beautiful. She had put her hands in her pockets three times so as not to run her fingers over the soft looking couch or the wallpaper that was simple lines of gray over white. Pretty cut-glass window panes were in the doors that looked out over the expansive yard. Sterling told her several times already that he was having the place worked on a little at a time because he'd been out of work for so long. But she loved every bit of it just the way it was.

"Myra, she's a friend of the witch that I was telling you about, she did a lot of the work for me." She asked him how that had happened. "I was having some issues and she wanted me safe. So, she asked if I would hire Alta. She's a witch too. Anyway, she wanted to expand the kitchen and did it."

"Just did it?" He nodded and told her that she did it magically. "I see. And what about this room? Did she do anything to this one? I mean, it's beautiful. She must have excellent taste. This is just what I'd want in a living room."

"She would have gotten it from your thoughts." Marty turned and looked at him when he answered her. "You see, this room wasn't finished when I left here this morning. The doors to the back were glass, but not stained glass like they are now. There wasn't any furniture in here either. Just a big pillow chair that I would drag from room to room when I was in them. Nor any curtains or lamps. There was a shelf, but all it had on it was empty pizza boxes that for some reason I never got around to taking out to the trash cans."

"You're telling me that she went into my head, pulled out what I liked, and made this room to suit me? That's just insane. I mean, not to mention a little creepy." He grinned and nodded. "Why do you find that funny?"

"Well, you have to admit that it's certainly easier than going to the store and picking something out that you might not like but that's all they had in stock." She told him he was missing the point. "Perhaps. But I'm glad that you like it this way. I do as well. You have excellent taste."

"I don't like you." She moved into the next area, the dining room, and he marveled at the changes in this one too. "I suppose this didn't look like this when you left either."

"No, it didn't. There weren't any built-in cabinets. Not even a table and chairs." He opened the doors to one of the cabinets and took out a glass that matched the place settings. "This is beautiful. I'm assuming that you've either owned this before or you've seen it."

"My grandmother had a few pieces to this set. She always wanted to find the rest of it but it was out of our reach. Why are you doing this to me?" He told her that he wasn't, but he loved what she'd done for him. "This is insane. I feel...I'm not sure I need to give you any more ammo, but I love this place and how it's altogether beautiful. But the fact that someone has been in my head.... I don't like that much."

"She means well. And I think she wanted to make a good impression on you because you're my mate. Nothing nefarious or anything like that. Just making you feel welcome." It wasn't a great answer but it was a good one. "Besides, as I said, it's beautiful. I love the changes. And they're good ones too."

She made her way around the dining room. The cabinets were filled with the set that she had grown up using. And they looked brand new, not fifty years old like her grandma's had been. Picking up one of the plates, she ran her hand over the design.

"She told me that they were a part of a set that she'd gotten from saving stamps. I had to look that up when she told me, but apparently, you could save up books of stamps and trade them in for merchandise. She wanted these dishes, the entire set, but that fad went out of business, and there just wasn't a great deal of extra money then for luxuries like this." He asked her how many she had. "Ten of the plates and bowls, and she was working on the salad plates and cups when they were broken. My mom—she was a drunk and a drug addict—broke a lot of them when she went on a rage. I think she's dead now too, but I don't know. I've not spoken to her or even heard from her since I was about four."

"I'm sorry." She nodded and put the plate back in the cabinet. "I can talk to Alta and ask her not to look into your memories. I'm not sure what will happen. I just let her do what she wants and it works out for us both. But if they're disturbing to you, I can ask her not to intrude."

"It's all right. I was just.... It's been a stressful few months. And having lost my job to someone like Bethany just topped it off." When he pulled her into his arms, she let him. Leaning back against his chest, Marty felt better than she had in weeks, maybe even months. As they stood there, neither of them talking, she looked around the room again.

The large dining table had a dozen chairs around it. They were oak, and she would bet that they were old too. She smiled when she remembered where she'd seen this set. It had been on a television show about the rich and famous, and she had fallen in love with it. Mostly because it meant a big family, but it was a nice set. There was a placemat at each seat that looked like it was

47

made of the finest linen.

"Mistress? There is a call for you on the house phone." Marty asked Alta who it was. "I believe it's one of the places that you applied for today. That man sure has a mouth on him. I've a good mind to seal it up for him."

"No, please don't do that." She stared at the woman. "Can you do that? I mean, really, can you seal up someone's mouth?"

"If they think they can talk to me that way, I will." Alta paused at the door and turned back to smile at her. "You don't let him talk to you that way either. There is no cause for him saying those things to anyone."

She went to the hall where the closet phone was and answered it. The man, she didn't know who, was speaking to someone in the room with him. Well, speaking wasn't quite right, but he was yelling obscenities at them. Marty told him to shut up.

"You will not talk to me that way, young lady. I've a good mind to have you arrested anyway. You've made my life a living hell, and I'm going to sue you for it." She asked him what she'd done. "You told my wife about Bethany. Do you know what she's doing to me now? My wife of twenty-three years is filing for divorce. And she'll get it too, thanks to you."

"I'm assuming this is Roger Dolan." He told her it damn well was and that he was pissed off. "Well, I think I figured that part out. How did you find me, anyway? Besides, even if I had thought of telling your poor wife, I don't know her well enough to do that. I'm not saying that I'm not glad that she knows, but I didn't do it. Perhaps you should talk to Bethany. She's just stupid enough to do something—"

"She's not stupid. She's delicate. And you'll not talk about her that way either. You should have been better at training her and perhaps she wouldn't have upset the Calhoun family. What the fuck were you thinking when you took that slice of pie from her and wouldn't let her serve it to them? And I found you by calling around. Someone saw you with them, and this number is the only one in the phone book." Sterling came to stand next to her so that he could listen in on the conversation. "Have you never learned that the customer is always right? That man has some large cash to throw around. Hell, his whole family is rich. And there you were treating them like some sort of shit off your shoes."

Sterling took the phone. "This is Sterling Calhoun." She heard Roger stutter and curse, then he asked if this was a joke. "No, no joke. Though I can see where you'd think it was. My brother related the entire thing to me. Not only did he say that Marty gave him the best service he'd ever had, but that Bethany, your bimbo, I guess, tried several times to take his food from him, and even changed his order around to suit herself. The lemons in his water, for one thing."

"She has this thing about lemons in her water. Why did he have to make a big deal out of that? Just take them off the glass and be done with it. There was no reason for him to make her feel bad." Marty laughed but stopped when Sterl put his hand over her mouth. "And the pie. She was just doing what the customer asked."

"Not true either, I'm afraid. Marty took the pie to the table only to have Bimbo try to take it back. She said that my sister-in-law could have it at the end of the meal, not the beginning, as she didn't like things messed up. In my opinion, I think I'd have just left that alone, but Bimbo wouldn't have it." Roger told him to stop calling her Bimbo. "Well, what would you call someone that singlehandedly pisses off enough customers that you might be out of business soon?"

"Mr. Mackey quit today, along with a few of the dishwashers. I don't even have enough people to work a shift, much less cook should anyone come in. And that's not my Bethany's fault. They said they wanted to work better hours." Sterling asked him if he

49

believed that. "Yes. People are fickle, and my Bethany is a good waitress."

"You go on believing that. And so you know, I'm going to marry Marty, and if you call here and threaten her again, I will make it my personal business to see you rot in hell." He put the phone back on the cradle slowly. Then he picked it up with the receiver and jerked it from the wall. She was staring at him when he tossed it across the room and it shattered. "I'd very much like to kiss you. Not a quick gentle kiss either, but I'd like nothing more than to consume you with it."

Nodding, she watched him walk toward her. It was stalking, pure and simple. And when he put his hand around her waist, Marty went to him willingly. His body fit against hers like it was made for it. Then he lowered his head to hers and kissed her.

~~~

Her touch did nothing to soothe his beast at first. Sterl was afraid of hurting her, but more afraid of scaring her. As he pulled her body flush to his, he could feel his wolf snarl at him. It was as if he was telling him to take her. Mark her.

When he lifted his head, he looked down at her and realized that she'd felt him too...his wolf was making her very aware of him. The gentle touch of her hand to his cheek calmed him in ways that Sterl hadn't ever felt before. That single touch let him take a deep breath and let it out slowly.

"I'm so sorry." Marty asked him for what. "I don't want to frighten you again. Nor do I want you to be afraid of me."

"I'm not. You're calm now, right?" He nodded. "Roger, he pissed you off. To be honest with you, I had no idea you could get that angry. You seem so laid back."

He kissed her again and then backed away enough that he could hold her hand. They continued through the house, and Sterl felt like he was calmer than he'd been since...well, forever, it seemed. Pointing out some of the changes of the house since she'd entered made them both laugh.

"Have you ever just, I don't know, thought of something outrageous and then checked to see if it was there?" He told her that he was just staying here for the most part, and not living in the house. "Well, that's sad. You have a lovely home, and you should enjoy it to the fullest. I would."

"You can." Sterl watched her face to see if she believed him or not. "This is our home now. Yours and mine. I want you to think of whatever you want in here. Make it for us."

"I don't know. We've only just met, and it is your house." He shook his head and opened the door to the master bedroom. He knew the moment she walked in that she'd come to realize her dreams really were coming true. "Oh, Sterling. It's beautiful."

Sterl hadn't slept in this room, mostly because the stairs had made him ache. But even after he'd been well, it had seemed like too much effort to come up here when all he wanted to do was lay his head on a pillow. The big pillow really had been his only means of sitting, and most of the time sleeping.

The room was so different, had he not been in it before, he would have thought it was with a different house. Even the colors in the room were perfect. Not dark and somber as he might have done, but bright, airy, and not too girlish. The bedspread alone made him think of warm nights snuggled with Marty. He loved the entire room now.

There had been two smaller windows in the room when he'd last been in here. Sterl liked the longer floor to ceiling ones that were on either side of the large four poster bed. There was a fireplace too, with a mantel over it that was large enough to hold a great many pictures. Walking deeper into the room, he saw that not only had the windows changed, but the dimensions of the room as well.

It was bigger, and the ceiling was taller. The single closet was gone now, to be replaced with two larger walk-ins. There were dressers in them and a connecting door. He loved the shoe shelf, the sweater bins, and the staggered hanging areas for longer as well as shorter clothing that needed to be hung up rather than put in a drawer.

The bathroom was spectacular. The long double sink was the length of the room. All marble, he thought, and the colors were outstanding, with gold and silver streaks running through it. A shower stall that would easily hold two people, as well as a claw-foot tub to the right of it, looked shareable. He saw a towel warming rack on the wall, as well as a linen closet that was filled with fluffy cream and blue towels, and soaps as well as other sundries in baskets with the names of the items on them. He picked up a bottle of the bubble bath on the little dresser near the tub and smelled it.

"Raspberries. I love this smell. Do you use it?" She nodded as she sat on the vanity chair that was in the middle of the sink. He was reasonably sure that it hadn't been there when they walked in. "You love this house, don't you?"

"Yes. Very much so. But I think we need to talk about a few things. Like, what do you expect from me? And where do you think this is going to go with us?" He asked her what she meant. "Well, I looked you up. There is some information about you, but not a great deal. I know that your family is one of the richest in the country, and you have a bit more than your family."

"I've invested well. And I have a nice pension from the school where I worked. But when I was hurt several years ago, I decided to live as cheaply as I could. I didn't have to, but I didn't want to get to the point where I was dipping into my money when there wasn't really a need for it. I also bought other properties when they were empty, and have been renting out a few homes in town to a few families. I've been too busy to play with being retired, so to speak, but I've only just figured out that I need to do that more; have fun I mean. I want to have fun and do things with you." She nodded. "As for the money being mine, I want you to understand something. It's ours. Everything is. Not just the money, but the house, any stocks I have, homes that I have as well. I own a car, but it's small and doesn't hold a lot. I had a truck, but I sold it to Noelle for her shop to haul things in."

She got up and left him there. He followed her to the bedroom and watched her walk to the window. He knew what she could see. Or thought he did. When he'd bought the house, one of the things that he liked most about it was the fact that there was a large pool and pool house. He'd not used it as much as he would have liked, but he would with Marty around, he thought.

"My grandma was all I had in this world. She was all right… not very huggy or even one to say that she loved me. I know she did. But she wasn't one to show her love, so in turn, I wasn't sure how to either." He didn't say anything. His family was the hugging type. They told each other that they loved them and meant it. And even in public, he'd hug his elders. "I don't know how to love you, Sterling."

That hurt him. Not for himself, but for her. She'd been stifled, he thought, in showing people her love, because no one had done it for her. Walking to her, he thought of all the things that he was going to enjoy with this woman. Living a long and happy life, one full of love, and holding her and making sure that she knew she was loved was going to be a priority.

"When I was ten or so, Mom took me to school. I don't remember why. I think I might have missed the bus or something. Anyway, as I was getting out of the car, she asked for a hug. My friends were there, all of them, and I told her no. I think it was the first time I'd ever told my mom no for any reason." He pulled her into his arms and looked out the window. The pool was still there but it was larger, and had a patio surrounding it that was wider than before. "When I got home that night, she was in the kitchen as she usually was, but she wasn't making dinner but sitting in her chair. Just sitting there. When I asked her if she was all right, she looked at me and I could tell she'd been crying. I asked her what was wrong."

Sterl thought of her face, the way that it had been slightly puffy, her eyes red from tears. She had touched a soft white hanky to her eyes and just stared at him. He hurt then and even now, thinking of how she had stared at him.

"She asked me what I would have done had she not been there that day. I wasn't sure what she meant, so she explained. Mom told me how she'd gone to school one day, just like normal, but she'd not been able to hug her daddy. She told me how she'd been too busy to stop by his room to tell him she loved him or give him a hug. He was working that day and got hurt. When she returned home, he had passed away." Marty looked up at him, her own tears falling now. "Since that day, I have made it a vow that I will never, for as long as I live, not hug someone because I'm too busy or too behind. I will touch you as much as I can. Show you in ways that you cannot imagine how much I love you. How much I love having you in my life, being a part of it with me."

"You love me?" Sterl told her that he loved her with all his heart. "You really do. I mean, you're not just saying that to get into my pants."

"No. But if you'd allow me to, I'd love to get you out of your pants."

She stared up at him, and he was ready to tell her that he'd been joking, just trying to lighten the mood, when she stepped back from him and started to unbutton her blouse.

"I've never seduced a man before." Sterl nodded. It was about all he could do at the moment with the sound of her voice making him hard, the thoughts of what she was about to show him making his head spin. "I've heard that women do it. But I've never been the type that men wanted to see.... Well, see naked."

"I do." He smiled when he realized how desperate he sounded. Even his voice had a pitch to it he'd not had since he'd been going through puberty. "Are you sure about this, Marty? Once I have you, there isn't any turning back."

"Yes, I'm aware of that. I'm a little frightened of you, not as your wolf or even you. But men in general. I don't have much confidence that they'll do the right thing by me." He sat down on the bed when she told him to. "You tell me if I'm doing this wrong in any way. All right?"

Christ, he thought to himself. She'd not even taken her blouse off, and he thought that if she got any better, he'd be dead. There already wasn't any blood in his head, all of it was centered right around his cock and groin. Adjusting himself enough to let off some of the pressure he could feel building, he watched her fingers move over the rest of the tiny little buttons and hoped that he'd be able to survive this. Otherwise, he was going to disappoint a few people when he keeled over dead.

Her blouse dropped from her fingers to the floor. Then she moved to the button snap and zipper of her pants. Sterl's mouth was dry, his body going between hot flashes of need to chills from seeing her for the first time. And when she had her jeans off, laying them atop the clothing she was discarding, he tried to swallow again and nearly bit off his tongue when she opened the front of her bra and her breasts were exposed. Christ, he really was going to die right here and now.

CHAPTER 5

Marty loved the way he was looking at her. It was sort of a cross between lust and hunger. No one had ever made her feel so desirable before, and she doubted very much if anyone would again. Just this man, the one before her, could love her like she wanted to be. Keep her safe as she'd never been able to do. And most of all, he would be the one that, no matter what, would cherish her.

"I love you, Sterling." He stood up then, pulling her into his arms. When he kissed her, she knew that this was right…the feelings that she had for him were true and everything that she'd hoped they'd be. "Now. Lie down. I'm going rock your world."

He sat and grinned at her. "You already have, love. Ever since the first time I saw you you've done nothing but rock my entire being. And to know that you love me only makes what we're about to do seem so perfect. It is perfect."

Marty was going to make this good. While she had no idea what it took to be sexy or even how to make him want her, she was going to rely on every trick she'd read in books. Most of it just meant letting him do all the work, but she was going to try and make him nuts with desire. And if the look on his face was any indication, she was pretty close to that already.

Slipping her bra down her arms, she held it over her breasts and watched his face. His gaze was intent on her body, her breasts. Taking it off and then dropping it to the floor with the rest of her clothing, she stood before him in her panties. Cupping her breasts in her hands, she tugged at her nipples and smiled at him.

"Do you like what you see?" He nodded. "Would you like to suckle at my breasts? How about taste my pussy? It's so wet right now."

Sterling was suddenly not there, and in his place was his wolf. And Christ almighty, what a wolf. She started to back away from him, not sure what had happened, when he growled low and took her hand in his mouth and nipped her. It hadn't really hurt but she was surprised by it. And afraid. He hadn't bared his teeth at her, but she could see the fur along his back standing on end.

He wants you. Marty shook her head. *Not to have sex. I'm sorry, honey. I truly am, but he wants to mark you. Taste you. He's a lot more aggressive than I am.*

"He's huge." The wolf laid down and whimpered. "I think he's beautiful. I've never thought of.... Are you sure he won't try and have sex with me?"

Yes. I'm sure. He just wants to taste all of you. Spread your legs and I promise you that he won't hurt you. She didn't know what to do, but when the wolf jumped off the bed, she backed up again. *He won't hurt you. Ever.*

She still wasn't so sure. But when he came to her, his head down and his body low to the floor, she watched him. Then he licked her ankle, knee, and then her thigh. It was warm and soft, his tongue. The texture of it made her wetter, the thought of him touching her with it, on her pussy, made her think this might not be too bad. When she opened her thighs for him, he moved slowly, his teeth, nipping a little hard at her skin but not enough to draw blood, making her dizzy with the need to come.

"What do I do?" Sterling told her to lay down on the bed. As she sort of stumbled to the bed, the wolf was right beside her. Her knees were wobbly and weak with need. "Now what?"

Take off your panties, or he can. She thought of that and didn't move. Would he tear at her skin too? Would he lick her through them if she didn't remove them? All the ideas and thoughts in her head were making her warmer, her body humming with a profound need. *Good. He'll love that too.*

His teeth pulled at the little straps at the side of her panties. When he yanked on the silky material, she nearly came at the sound of it tearing. Then before she could ask what she would have to do now, the wolf was licking her from gate to clit and causing her to scream out a quick release. Holy Christ, this was much better than she could have imagined.

The wolf licked her to completion so many times that she was woozy with it. Every time she thought that she'd had enough, he would nip at her thigh, her pussy, or even her knee and she'd come again. Sliding his tongue into her, fucking her with it, he made her scream so many times that she was hoarse with it. Ready to faint with pleasure, she looked up when Sterling touched her.

"He might have killed me. I don't think I have anything left in me to make love with you." Sterling grinned at her. "I'm serious. I'm done. I'm sorry, but I don't think—"

Sterling filled her. It wasn't painful, him taking her, but he simply filled every part of her body when he slid his cock inside of her pussy. Holding him, just keeping her hands tightly gripped to his arms, she looked up at him and felt his love pour over her. He hadn't moved, not once, but she could see on his face what it was costing him not to do so.

"I need to make love to you, darling. To make you mine as my wolf has done. Fill you with my seed so that we'll be one." She nodded, her eyes filling with tears at the way his voice seemed to caress her. "I love you, Marty. Every day, I'll love you more for as long as I live."

He made love to her. Not just her body, but her heart and her mind as well. Each time he moved deep into her, he kissed her. His tongue traced her chin and her ear. Marty wrapped her legs around his, riding upwards when he came down into her. And when he nipped at the pulse at her throat, Marty didn't care if he tore into her now. In fact, it seemed the most natural thing in the world for her to offer herself to him.

"Come." The single word brought her body up off the bed, her heart sputtered to a stop, and she was sure that her blood had heated to a volcanic temperature. And when Sterling bit down on her throat, instead of pain, she felt connected. Her mind open to his as Sterling's was to hers. She came to be centered, her life complete for the first time. And Marty knew a love so deep that she couldn't imagine being without it.

Childhood memories. Hurts and pain. The she-devil the night that she'd marked him. The people he'd watched being killed. The witch, Chris Bentley. Myra, the second to Chris. His mother, his dad, all his family were there as well. The day that the demon had come to them, taking away not just his nightmares but his need to die. She felt his sorrow at life. His need to stop breathing, and the love that he had for her and his family. And then she came.

Stars. Rainbows. Flowers. They danced behind her eyelids for several seconds until her body started to function again. Her vison blurred, then she snapped out.

Waking, the room was darker. The fireplace was roaring in the room, and was the only light. Rolling to her side, she was pulled closer to Sterling, his arms wrapped around her, and he snuggled into her neck. Marty wasn't sure she'd ever been this comfortable before. Not in a very long time anyway. Wrapping her arms around his, she laid there and thought of spending her life with this man, and thought there couldn't have been anything better than that.

"You're very wonderful to wake next to." Marty rolled to her back and looked up at him. The wolf was there, his eyes glowing back at her from Sterling's face. "I love you."

"I can see him. Your wolf. I think I might love him as well." Sterling kissed her, taking her breath away with just the simple touching of their lips. "I've never spent the night with anyone before. What do we do when we wake in the middle of the night?"

"Make love again? However, as much as I'd love to take you several more times before the sun comes up, I'm starving. I bet you are as well." Her belly growled loudly. "I'm going to take that as a yes. Let's go raid the kitchen, and perhaps I can find someplace to fill your other needs as well while we're at it."

"You're on." They got up and she realized she had nothing to wear here. Sterling told her to look in the closet or dresser for something of his. She walked into the big room and stopped. "Sterling? There's women's clothing here that wasn't before."

"I bet it fits you too." Marty ran her fingers over the blouses that were hung on padded hangers. The drawers were filled with bright and colorful sweaters. Opening the drawer to the big dresser in the middle of the room, she squealed with delight. Sterling joined her in the room. "What did you...? Christ, knowing that you're going to be having that on under your clothing is going to keep me in a constant state of arousal. Try one of them on."

The bra and panty set was beautiful. Sensual too. The bra was a dark green lace, and her breasts felt supported yet sexy too. Sterling moved his fingers over the lace and looked at her. She moved back so that she could pull on the panties before he tore them off her.

"It's beautiful. I've never had anything so nice before. I usually buy my things at the local department store, but this...I'm betting this is more than I made in a week in tips during the holiday season." He smiled and sat on the bench in the room. "There are about a dozen sets like this. And look, the ones I took out? They've been replaced by another set. Oh Sterling, this is amazing."

They dressed quickly then. Sterling went to his part of the closet to dress while she lingered over which sweater to pull on. It was like Christmas for her, having so many things, beautiful things to choose from. As they made their way to the lower level, Sterling held her hand and Marty felt absolutely wonderful.

The refrigerator was full of things to snack on. She had thought that Alta had left it for them, but Sterling said that it was the house again. It was there to anticipate needs. She thought she could get used to this, having her every whim taken care of. There would be drawbacks, she knew, but for now, she was happy and content. As they were eating a cheeseball and crackers while Sterling made them sandwiches, Alta joined them and started fussing at Sterling.

"You should have called me. I would have fixed you something hot to go in your bellies." He told her that he had it, she should go back to bed. "I don't sleep. Too old now to take the habit up. There is just too much to see and do to be lying about in a bed that has to be done up all the time. Besides, I love cooking for you, but having a missus here, this will be the best thing for this old witch."

They ate ham and eggs, fluffy homemade biscuits, and gravy. By the time she was pushing her plate away, Marty thought she might bust. And when Alta shooed them out of the kitchen, Sterling picked her up in his arms and carried her back to bed. She was too exhausted to protest.

~~~

Noelle was setting up a display on one of the tables she'd gotten in a few days ago when Sterl and Marty came in. Smiling, she looked at them. They were in love. It shined off them like sunlight. She was so happy for them and the future they'd have. And Noelle was going to get a good friend out of this too.

"Coming to work, Sterl?" He said that he had some paintings to pack up. "All right. If you'd like to hang out with me, Marty, I'm sure he won't be too long. I have no one to talk to, so the distraction will be nice."

"What is it you're doing?" Noelle explained to her that she'd been collecting furniture and things from vampires and other older creatures and helping them make a buck or two. "That's nice. I would imagine that they'd have a lot of things from over the years."

Noelle finished the display and wandered over to where Marty was looking at a desk. "It came in a few days ago. I'm not sure what I can do with it yet. It doesn't have a chair that works under it, and there are several stubborn drawers that I can't get open. I think it belonged to a large estate, but the person who brought it by just dumped it by the back doors and didn't leave any kind of reference for it. I'm almost afraid to sell it because they might be back for it, but Chloe said that I should go ahead since I reported it here. What do you think of it?"

"It's called a bootlegger's desk." She moved to the side of it and ran her fingers along the top. "I took a few classes in college that dealt with antiques. There is usually a small button to open — Here it is."

Noelle looked in the drawer when it opened, then at Marty. The expression on her face was exactly how she felt. Shocked. Fear. Excitement. All the things one would expect when they opened a drawer with a gun and lots of cash in it.

"Don't touch anything." Noelle said she wouldn't. "I don't know what all this means, but I'm reasonably sure that it's not good. I mean, these are one hundred dollar bills, and it looks like the date is from the thirties."

"There's a book too. Do you suppose it has a name in it?" She realized she was whispering, as did Marty when she told her she didn't know. "We have to call someone. I was thinking Tanner. He's an attorney."

"All right, but no one else. I mean, I've talked to Sterling's family and they can't keep a secret to save their lives." Noelle laughed, then covered her mouth. "This is some serious shit here. I wish now that I'd not shown you."

"What about the other drawers?" Marty moaned and she laughed again. "We've already opened one of them. We might as well do the rest."

"But after Tanner comes here. We need a witness, I think." For what, they had no idea, but Noelle agreed with her. "Also, just for now, I think we should just close this and hope that it doesn't open again. I was just showing off, I think. I never dreamed that it would be like this."

"I'm glad that you did it. I would have hated to have sold this to someone and find out that I gave away riches that might belong to someone else." Marty said they were more than likely from some honest to goodness bootlegger. "That's what I was thinking too."

Tanner arrived about twenty minutes later. They'd not told him what they needed him for, but lucky or unlucky for them, TJ was with him. This man could and did talk a mile a minute, but right now, as he peered in the first drawer, he was speechless.

"We need the police." Marty said nothing, but Noelle asked him what they'd do. "Well, they need to be involved in the event that this is stolen or illegal money. I'll call Chloe and see what she can tell us. Being family and the chief of police, we know she can be trusted."

Noelle was glad they'd been able to convince her sister-in-law to take the job with the police department. It had been a while since anyone had been trustworthy in the place, and now that most of the people working there had been taken to prison, things were going much smoother. Most, if not all, of the police had been hitmen that were working for the former chief, and had been taken down by the Feds. Anastasia, one of the agents that Chloe had called, had been helping her find good, trusted men to fill the positions as well.

The book was removed by Chloe, and everything they did was being recorded. TJ was helpful in that as he had his phone ready. Noelle had to tell Elijah; he had felt her fear and had decided to come by to watch the proceedings rather than have her tell him about them. After they opened the second drawer and began the inventory on it, the entire family was there, including Sterl. It was becoming a fun affair really, with everyone having their own version of what had transpired to have so much money in the desk. She thought that Jasmine's was the best and more than likely most truthful.

"I think that some old gangster had this desk, and he hid the money away so that his men wouldn't find it. His wife would have known, but maybe she died before he did. Then no one, for many years, wanted it, so this poor old desk sat in storage somewhere until they opened the space and found it. And that book? All those people there are more than likely gone as well, or even too old to remember the man, much less this desk."

"I'll see what I can find out with these names. For all we know, they might live right here in town, or close enough that they might have a claim on this money." Noelle thought that was unlikely. "I know you said that you have records of who brought you what, but you said that this was just at the back door of the place the other day, so we have to make every effort to find them, just in case they claim later that we stole it from them."

They'd counted the money four times. It was just under two hundred thousand dollars in cash. But there were other things to consider too. The book with some sort of code in it, jewels and loose diamonds in a felt bag that weighed about three pounds, gold bars, three of them, with the Treasury Department stamp on them, as well as deeds to several pieces of property and a book for a bank in Europe. Noelle didn't want to have to be the one to search for what would basically, from the dates in it, be a hundred-year-old bank account.

Marty showed them what she'd found when she looked for a maker's mark. The woman knew a great deal more than she did about furniture, and Noelle was going to ask her to be her partner when this was cleared up. For now, they all watched her as she showed them not only the manufacturer, in this case a single-family name, but also the year it had been made. Nineteen-twelve.

"I was going to put it with the things that we have for the resale items. I had no idea that it was so old." Noelle ran her fingers over the inlaid top of several different kinds of wood. "I bet when this was brand new it was so beautiful."

"It would be easy to clean up and made to look good." James looked at the desk with Scott and they determined that it only needed some love. "I think we can bring her back to her old self with a little stripper and some polish. You let me know when we can start on it and I'll do it. I'm thinking that I'll look it up, some way to make it pretty again without hurting the finish on those woods. Might even be able to name a few more of them by then too."

"I want it." They all turned to Jasmine when she spoke. "I'll buy it off you, but I want it for my house. I love it. And it's so lovely that I think it would look very special in my office. You tell me a price and I'll pay it."

Noelle wouldn't charge her anything, but she was sure that she'd not take it then. They'd talk later, she thought. When there was less going on. Christ, so much had happened since Marty came in with Sterl.

Just before she closed the doors for the day, Sterl came down again from his studio. She was glad to have him working up there. It gave her a little bit of security knowing that a wolf was up there all the time. As well as now that he had a mate, she had constant company. Marty hung around with her the entire day, each of them making the displays prettier by just bouncing ideas off each other. Noelle asked Sterl what he was doing with his paintings as they were counting out the day's cash.

"I have a gallery opening in two weeks, but don't tell anyone." She sat down and glanced at Marty when she sat beside her. "I'm not sure if this is a good idea or not, but I don't want the family to know so they can tease me about it when it's a flop."

"It won't be a flop. I've told you that." Marty patted him on the back when he sat down and spoke to her. "He has it in his head that no one will show up, and that those that do will think him too deranged. I think they're very powerful paintings. The two that he has at the house are something that you have to look at several times to see it all. And even then, I'm betting that I missed something."

"How many do you have?" She had to ask him to repeat himself when he said two dozen. "You've been painting a lot then. I want to go to the opening. Please? I won't tell anyone there that you're my brother-in-law, but I so want to go. And I think you should tell your family, too. I doubt anyone would be making fun of you."

"Grandma knows. She's the one that set this up. I think this guy owed her a favor or something. He said that I'd sell out the first night of it. I hope that Grandma isn't buying them to make me feel good." Noelle thought she'd do that, Jasmine was a very kind hearted woman, but she wouldn't do that to Sterl. At least she hoped that she wouldn't. She'd be too afraid that he'd find out, and it would hurt her for him to feel that way. "Anyway, the gallery opening is in two weeks. I have to be there, but Isaac said that I didn't have to let anyone know who I was unless I wanted to. All my work is signed with just an S."

She wanted to beg him to see his work. Sterl had been so quiet about what he was doing up there, just coming in and painting at all hours. Sometimes here before her and leaving after she did for the day. And now she found out that he had a gallery wanting his work. Noelle was so excited that she wanted to hug him, but she knew that of all the brothers, Sterl was the hardest to get to know, and she didn't want to embarrass him. She thought it had to do with what that monster had done to him.

"See? I told you that you should tell your family. They'd be as proud of you as I am. And if not, I'd kick their asses." They all laughed when Marty spoke. "How about we have them over for dinner tonight and tell them then? You know as well as I do that as soon as they find out, they're not going to be happy with you for not telling them before."

"I know, but I don't want to look like a failure in their eyes. I've been a pain in the ass for a while now, and I don't need to have them feeling sorry for me any longer." He took Marty's hand in his and kissed the back of it before continuing. "If they make fun of me or tease me in any way, I'm going to blame it all on you."

"Deal." They both laughed and Noelle was glad. Then it occurred to her what else was in two weeks.

"What's the date of your opening?" He told her. "That's pretty close to Thanksgiving. We'll have to make hotel reservations now or we won't have anywhere to stay. And maybe while we're at it we could all have dinner together, sort of bring in the holidays like that. I mean, it's the Friday before turkey day, so we could even get a bit of shopping in as well."

Her mind was working out details as they sat there. Not only would they need a hotel, but dresses too. Noelle was getting large enough now that people could tell that she was pregnant, and she was happy about that, as well as being proud of having twins. As they worked out when they were going to leave, she started making notes on what to take with them. This was going to be so much fun, and she had no doubt that Sterl was going to be a great success.

CHAPTER 6

Sterl wasn't sure what to think. The showing was in a week, and all his work was sitting out where anyone could see it. They'd been asked to come by the gallery to see if the placement of his paintings were all right with him. It was scary to think that he was going to have people judge him in seven days. As he held onto Marty's hand, he tried to calm his wolf. They were both freaking out a little. Marty stopped him and grabbed his chin, making him look at her.

"Breathe." He nodded. "No, you're not breathing. You're doing this short pant thing that is going to make you pass out. Take a breath in and let it out slowly. Come on, do it."

He did as she told him, but it wasn't helping. He was dizzy with anxiety and sick to his stomach. When she snapped her fingers in front of his face, he let out the breath that he'd not realized he was holding and looked at her.

"They hung them up." She pointed out that's what they did in a gallery. "I know that, but these are mine that they hung up all over the place."

"Again, that's what they do when they have a spectacular artist. Did you really expect they'd hide them under great big sheets and have people guess what was under them? Like that show...the one where you have to pick a door. Remember that one?" He told her that he didn't like her right now. "You love me, and you also know that I'm right. Don't think of it as your work and look around. It looks lovely, don't you think?"

They were displayed nicely. The four that he'd done at his bleakest time were hung in order of his painting them. They were good looking paintings until you got close enough to see what was really hidden in them. The darkness of that night and the following hours were right there for anyone to see. A Nightmare on Canvas was what his grandma had called them when asked the series name. Sterl thought that it was perfectly named because that was just what it was. A nightmare.

There were other paintings, just as dark as the first set was, in this room as well. There was the she-devil that he'd painted one night when he'd seen her face in his dreams. Other paintings were spread out over the gallery, hanging on walls of white so as not to distract from their beauty. One set showed the way he'd felt, his body torn up, his mind a turmoil of the thoughts that had been there from her. Then there was the last set of paintings.

These he had called Redemption. The five paintings were lined up so that they made one continuous picture. There was the oak tree in the middle, its roots going deep within the pits of hell. The demon took up one whole canvas to the right, his body filling some of the space in the one next to it, and there was little doubt that this man was from somewhere not of this earth. The dagger lay at the feet of someone, but their faces were blurred so that no one would know that it was his brothers. He hadn't done that consciously, but his heart had done it so that no one would ask questions of them, or him for that matter.

The other two, including one of the she-devil, were on the left. These frightened him the most. One was of her, her body white as a ghost and her long flowing hair wrapped around the man in front of her. It wasn't what had happened, but it seemed fitting to show that she had control over one of them. Mostly him.

72

The painting to the left was of hell, or at least his interpretation of it. There were bodies there, some of them entwined in sexual positions that defied any kind of imagination, except for his. He stared at this one, knowing that on some level it was as true as anything else that had happened to him that day.

Then, within the liquid looking blood red water, there were bodies. Faces of people that had been taken there for one reason or another. Blurred, so no one could tell who they were or if they were someone that they knew. He'd done that too, on purpose, but he could name a few of them. He supposed in some morbid way people would see who they wanted, put faces to the people there to feel some sort of satisfaction in their life. Sterl saw only one, and thankfully she could no longer bother him and his family.

The parents of the she-devil were there as well. He had no idea why their faces had come to him when he'd been painting this. Also, the people that had, over the centuries, come to the aid of Helenia, the creature that had nearly killed him. Sterl stared at them, all those people that had been as much a part of his nightmares as the woman herself.

"There is a great deal of interest in this series." He looked over at Isaac when he spoke quietly. "I used a part of it, only a small glimpse of it, to put on the fliers. There have been a couple of dozen calls to my office from people asking to see the rest of it. I haven't answered them except to say the show dates and times. This alone should bring in a great many people. I need to ask you, because there are as many questions as there are reasons you gave me to remain at a distance from this. But are you still going to remain private?"

"Yes. I'm not sure what people will say, and I'm a little overwhelmed by this." Isaac said he could understand that. "My family is going to come too. I had to tell them. They're coming into town in a couple of days to do some shopping. They don't want to come to the gallery until the night of the showing. To be honest with you, I'm not sure I want them here at all."

"I'm sure that they'll be supportive of you." He frowned and Sterl asked him what was wrong. "My brother is giving me a hard time. I don't know what to do about him. I told you that he's been fired, but he's scaring my family a little, especially my wife."

"I'm sorry to hear that. Is there anything I can do?" Sterl wasn't sure what he could do, but he'd help the man if possible. "I can have someone come and guard your family if you'd let me. I have some very persuasive friends."

"You mean the vampire? Or the pack?" He told him both. "Noah came by the other day. He was very helpful in helping us set this up. Your grandmother called him, I guess, and told him what was going on with my brother. I had no idea that Robert could be so destructive."

Grandma had told him about how Isaac's brother had tried to destroy some work that had been brought in a few weeks ago. Not his, but things that were set to go into the gallery from local artists. Robert had taken an axe to some of the boxes the work had arrived in, but lucky for everyone, the merchandise had already been removed. But the back door and a few other items hadn't been so lucky.

"You just say the word and I can have men watching your family as well as the gallery." He told him that he'd like his family watched over. "Anything. I don't know what this will bring you, this showing of mine, but I owe you so much for taking me on."

"We're both going to be very happy at the end of this. I'm positive. One of your paintings is already sold, as you know, and the rest will as well. And any time you get more work done, give me a call and we can work out something again. This is the best art we've had in here for a very long time." Sterl wasn't so sure about that, but he thanked him.

Marty joined him just as he was moving to the room where the last of his work was hanging. It seemed such a waste to him, to have his paintings spread out all over the big building. Isaac had told him it was to have a better showing. Give people the opportunity to gather it all in before going to the next work. Marty kissed him quickly and stood in front of the painting simply called Death.

"I love this one, by the way." He asked her why. "I'm not sure how to explain this, but it's like you've looked deep into my soul, all my nightmares and memories, and put them here." Sterl looked at the painting while she continued to explain. "See, when you look here, you see the flowers and roses nodding in the sunlight. But it's not there, it's an illusion. The roses are really blood splatters. The flowers are the print on the dress that the woman who has been killed is wearing. The trees look to be in the full bloom of fall, but they too are covered in blood. This place where it looks like it's a picnic, it's really a covering for the other deaths. You've created what should be a nice family outing and made it a horrific murder scene."

"I don't know where this came from." She nodded. "When I started painting this one, I saw just what you started to see at first. Then the paint seemed to take on a different scope. The deaths of the people were there, but not until you looked hard enough to see them."

"Yes, I see that. You're very good at that. You give the first impression of it being a nice normal picture, then as you look at it, you can see more and more of what really is going on. Like that knife." He looked where she was pointing and he nodded, asking her about it. "I've seen this painting twice now, and I've only just seen the knife sticking from the basket. That's scary to think that these people were killed by the very blade that they brought with them to have a bit of cheese with."

The two of them wandered around the gallery. There was

other work in the rooms with his, but not many pieces. Soft art, Isaac had called it, to give the viewer a little bit of a break. Marty told him what she'd discovered when she'd been working with Noelle for the last few days. He knew she was trying to relax him a little, and loved her all the more for it.

"She's very good at what she does. Did you know that?" He said that he did. "She wants me to travel with her for a few weeks. I guess she's worried about doing much more after the New Year. I don't blame her. Not with the babies coming and all. And she said that I could teach her a few things that I learned in college. Which, now that I brought it up, I do want to finish."

"And you should. Take as many classes as you need, so long as you aren't too tired when you come home at night to be with me. But about Noelle. I'm glad that the two of you are working in the shop. She's busy all the time now, but I think she still gets lonely. I know I would. And she's getting tired more often now. Carrying twins would be very hard on her. She's so small." They were at the front of the building when he looked out. "How about I take you to the diner over there, we go back to the hotel, and I ravish your body? That way I can take a nap before I have to come back here to pose for pictures."

"I heard that Isaac wants you to be all pretty for this." Sterl groaned. "Yes to all of that, by the way. I had to go do a little shopping for some nicer under things. The dress that was provided by the house, it didn't have anything like that with it."

"I'm thinking that it meant for you go naked under it." She stopped so suddenly he took several steps before turning to look at her. "I was kidding, love. I'm sure that it forgot."

"No. I think you're right. The way that it's cut.... Yes, I do believe that you're right. I'm to go naked under the dress." He was the one left behind when she started walking again. "Wait until you see it. It's so nice that you.... Where are we going?"

He had grabbed her hand and was dragging her back to the

hotel. The thought of her naked anywhere was enough to make him stone hard. But he wanted to see this dress, or perhaps her naked self that was going to be under it. As soon as they entered the hotel and got their messages, he took her to the elevator and kissed her even as the doors were closing behind them. Sterl wasn't sure they were going to make it to the room at this rate.

~~~

Marty was holding her clothing to her body as they sprinted to their room. Sterling had torn buttons from her blouse, broken the hooks on her bra, and had ripped her pants down one side to her knee. Not that his clothing fared any better.

She'd tried to be careful with his shirt, but once he bit her in the throat, all bets were off. Marty could only think of one thing, having him inside of her as soon as possible. She almost felt sorry for the guy watching the camera monitors. There was a camera in every elevator, she'd noticed, and wondered briefly how often he got a peep show.

As soon as he had the door to their room unlocked, she was naked. When he pressed her to the door and told her not to move, she had only a second to realize what he was going to do. His large wolf was at her pussy, bringing her to peak twice before she had to hold onto the wall behind her.

Her knees were weak, her body spent, but he didn't stop as she slid to the floor. Her legs were nudged open by his large head and he continued to devour her as she fell to the floor on her back. Even after coming so many times she'd lost track, as soon as Sterling was over her, his body pressing into hers, she knew that she needed more.

"I love you." He kissed her then, showing her with more than words that he did truly love her. "Will you marry me soon, today if I can manage it?"

"Yes, and I'll love you forever." He took her then, filled her with his cock over and over until she was screaming out her need.

Then he licked her throat, and she knew that this was going to be it for her. And as soon as he bit down on her, Marty came apart for one final time before she passed out completely.

Upon waking she realized something was wrong. Rushing to the bathroom, she saw Sterling bent over the commode throwing up. Touching his back with her hands, she offered him comfort in the only way she knew how. She told him he was going to be fine and that she loved him.

"I can't do this." She asked him what he meant. "Go through with this opening. What the fuck was I thinking? I can't go there and hear what people think of my work."

"Why do you care?" He looked at her and asked her what she meant. "Are you going to stop painting if they don't sell? Is this going to be all you ever do with your talent?"

"I don't think I can. It's like a salve over open wounds." She nodded and sat on the floor with him. "You're making a point that I'm trying my best to understand. But my head is pounding with terror and my heart is beating about ten million times a second."

"No one knows who you are as a painter but your family, correct?" He nodded and leaned back against the tub after flushing the commode. "Do you remember what your family said when you told them that night? How they were so proud of you for doing something that you were good at? I don't think they would have cared if you were good or not so long as you were happy. Am I right on that too?"

"My family has always been supportive in everything I do. As they are with the rest of them. But again, I don't understand where you're going with this." Marty grinned. "Are you trying to tell me that I'm being stupid for worrying about this?"

"No. God no. What I'm telling you is that you go to this opening with an open mind and hang around with your family. And if you're really good, I know where the closet is that has a nice lock on the door where I can distract you." He smiled. "There you are. And I'll tell you something else. I have a good idea that you're going to walk away from this with a great deal of praise, as well as more people wanting all of your work than you ever imagined."

"Why?" She asked him what he meant. "Why is it you think that I'm going to be successful at this? I mean, these paintings are of nightmares. Mine and my family's. There are things in them that will haunt me for the rest of my life. Why is it you think that anyone is going to want them in their homes?"

"Because I think that there are more people out there having the same sort of nightmares, the same fear that haunts them daily, and no way of dealing with it. You, Sterling Calhoun, showed them that in your pain that they can find an outlet. That there is hope for them. Not necessarily in painting, but something else, something they might not even be good at, but like you said, a salve over an open wound. And not only that, but you can give them something more to focus on than their own pain for a little while." He nodded and leaned his head back against the glass doors of the shower. "You can do this, Sterling. I know that if anyone can, it'll be you. You might even find that not only are you good as an artist, but people won't be harsh to you."

"What if someone figures it out? That I painted them? That it's me in those paintings?" She told him not to borrow trouble where there wasn't any yet. "I'm not borrowing trouble, love. I'm just trying to be realistic."

"No, you're trying to convince yourself that no one will want them, and you already know that some people have already been interested in your work." He laughed. "What is it now, big guy?"

"Are you always this supportive?" Marty told him she'd never had anyone that loved her before. "Good answer, but not answering my question."

"No. Usually I'm the one that stays back out of harm's way

and lets the world go on around me. Regardless of the outcome too, I'm willing to go with the flow of things so no one notices me." He pulled her to him and she laid her head on his shoulder. "Now, we have things to do today that are not going to get done while we sit here. I need to go shopping for some gifts for your family, and you have some contracts to sign with Isaac. Who, by the way, I really like."

"I do as well." Neither of them moved to get up. "A few months ago, Myra came to me and told me that someone was coming into my life that would mean a great deal to me. I thought it would have been you, but she assured me that it was a male. I think she was talking about Isaac. He has come to mean a great deal to me."

"He is very special to me as well. Did I tell you that he helped me out with this dress by sending his wife to help out? She's amazing...Gloria is her name, and their little boy's name is Benson. He's adorable as well." Sterling finally stood up and helped her to stand. "Are you okay now? I mean, do I have to beat you around a little to get you in a better frame of mind?"

"No. I think I'm going to be all right now." He hugged her to his body and she was warmed by it. "I truly love you, Marty. And you and I are going to get married as soon as I can arrange it."

"Good. I need you to be a permanent fixture in my life."

She turned on the water in the shower and he pulled out his kit to shave. They'd both have to come back here before the opening, but for now they were going to enjoy the day. She really did want to get some shopping done before his family arrived.

Her cell was ringing as she came out of the bedroom.

"This is Robert Sullivan. I'm trying to reach someone by the name of Calhoun. I don't have a first name." Marty told him she was a Calhoun. It wasn't true yet, but it mattered little in the larger scheme of things. "The painter? If so, then you're the one that I need to talk to. I want you to pull your art from the gallery now."

"Why would I do that?" He laughed but didn't explain. "I know who you are. You're the brother of Isaac. He said that you were scaring his family and had done some terrible things to his work. We've been working with him on this opening, and we've become good friends."

"I don't really care what you think Isaac is doing for you, but you should know that he's a cheat and a womanizer." She laughed at the stupidity of the comment. "You don't believe me? Well, he threw me out of the building for no reason. He's even gone so far as to keep me from my sister-in-law and niece."

"You have a nephew, not a niece, and it was my understanding that you threatened them. And you tried to destroy the art that was a part of an exhibit." He told her that he'd been upset for being fired. "That's more than being upset, it's nastiness on your part. Why do you think I should take the paintings from the gallery? Are you going to do something to the building?"

"I've had enough of him and his rules. He was supposed to keep me on as a favor to our mother, but he fired me for no good reason. And even if he had one, I'm his brother and he should have let it all go. Sometimes I think he's just doing this to get back at me for being the smarter of the two of us." Marty asked him how he'd come to that conclusion. "Have you seen some of the work he has in there? Why, none of it is going to bring him much in the way of money. And we all know that's what makes the world go around. And that's another thing, he stopped paying me."

"Well, if you don't work there, you really shouldn't expect to be paid, now should you?" He said that he did. "Well, I guess it really sucks to be you then. Get yourself a job, don't bring prostitutes to work, and try to keep your nose clean. That's the best advice that I can offer you."

"I want you to pull the paintings you have in there. I want him to fail." She told him no just as Sterling came out of the bedroom. Putting the phone on speaker, she let him listen in. "You're going to regret this. I was going to pay you dearly for them."

"You just told me that you hadn't been paid. Where are you supposed to get this money you're telling me about?" He told her that he'd been stealing for a long time. "You mean from your brother and the artists that are in the gallery?"

"Not that anyone missed any of it. But yes, both were good resources for ready cash. Why not? And if he'd not barred me from coming into the building, I would have stolen some of yours as well. You see, I'm doing you a favor by not stealing from you, so you should compensate me so we can both make some money." She looked at Sterling when he laughed. "Are you making fun of me? I don't think that's very nice when I'm trying to talk to you. Honey, you have no idea what sort of money I can come up with by stealing and then reselling things in that place."

"Oh really? Well, I guess it's a good thing you can't get in there anymore. And yes, as a matter of fact, I am laughing at you. You're insane. Not to mention lazy and a thief, as well as an idiot." Robert told her that he resented her calling him an idiot. "But the rest of it, you're fine with that?"

"Of course. It's all true, so why deny it?" He laughed and Marty looked at Sterling, who was shaking his head. "So, by this I'm assuming that you're not going to take your work from the gallery? It's too bad really. I think we could have come to like each other. I know that I could have made a bit of cash off you. But now I guess you'll have to be dealing with me after he fails. Sullivan is a respected name in the art world, as you know. But I wouldn't expect to get any money from me. I have expenses, and once I'm the owner, as I should have been, then you will be shit out of luck." He closed the connection after that.

"He's nuts." Sterling laughed. "I mean, like really off his

rocker nuts. Why is he admitting that he's not only a thief but also a blackmailer? And he even admitted that he wasn't going to pay us should he ever be in charge of the gallery. He needs someone to keep an eye on him before he hurts someone. Namely, Isaac and his family."

"I agree, and I've spoken to Trent. He's going to put a few more pack around the Sullivan home, as well as the gallery. He said that he has his best man on Isaac too." She told him what he missed from the early part of the call. "Why do you think he thought you'd just turn them over to him? I mean, really? How does he even make that work out in his head?"

"I don't know, but I think we need to be ready for about anything tonight at the preopening. He's not going to go away nicely." Sterling said he didn't think so either. Marty had no one she could call in to help them, but she was going to be ready. This wasn't going to go well, she thought.

CHAPTER 7

TJ loved dressing up. He'd had a tux in his closet since he'd been married, just waiting for a time or event to wear it. This one, he thought, was going to be one of his proudest moments. Only second to him marrying the love of his life. He fussed with his tie again, and then decided that he was handsome enough and went to the sitting area in their hotel room. His Christine was there waiting for him, and she looked beautiful.

"Well? Do you think that I look all right?" He asked her to turn for him. "Oh, TJ, I want this to be wonderful for him, and I'd hate to look bad."

"If you looked any better, my dear, we'd not be leaving this room until much later." She flushed. "We might not anyway. Come here and let me help you out of that beauty."

"You will not muss me, Trent James, or so help me, I'll knock your noodle off." She came to him anyway and smiled when he kissed her. "You look good yourself. I love that we're going to be going there in style, don't you?"

"Yes. Oh, my goodness. I nearly forgot." He ran back to his luggage and came back with a box for her. "I got this for you. I had an idea that you'd be as pretty as ever, but I wanted you to have a bangle to think of me when you're out and about."

He'd found the little antique store right across from the hotel

85

where they were staying yesterday when they arrived. He'd had it in his head to look at prices of things, to see how they were faring on dressing up some of the items that they had for sale, but he'd glanced only for a second in the jewelry case and the bracelet had caught his eye.

The man had told him that it was from the thirties or before. He had no idea since he'd not been able to find a mark on it, but TJ had. It had been from the roaring twenties, and not only that, but the jeweler's mark was one that he'd seen on a great many pieces that came in little blue boxes. He told her what he'd been able to find out about the piece. He was almost as excited to tell her what he'd found as he was wrapping her up in the treasure.

"It was made for a man that wanted to give it to his mistress. His wife, from what I could find out, was suffering from depression and the man had to have her committed. According to the story that was online, she'd lost their baby about a year after they were married and she never recovered." Christine told him that was a sad story. "That part is, yes, but let me finish it. The mistress, a very beautiful woman, had given him all that she was. They couldn't marry, of course, not with his wife so ill, but he was happy. Then about a year or so after she moved in with him, she gave him a son."

"Oh, how lovely. And they lived happily ever after?" He told her they hadn't, but that wasn't the best part. "TJ, I don't know if you're aware of this, but this is not a good thing that you're telling me. It's depressing me as well."

"Let me finish. You'll love it at the end, I promise you. Anyway, they didn't have the best of time of it. She was demanding and shrill when she realized that he was never going to marry her. And that the money was all tied up in medical bills and other things. Then one night, in a fit of rage, she left him and the boy. This man, he was devastated, and when he went to see his wife the next time, he brought the boy and confessed all. She looked at him for the first time in four years and asked for the child." Christine frowned at him, so he hurried to the end of the tale. "She took one look at that child and declared him to be her son. She got better after that, looking forward to her son and husband coming to see her every day. Then after a few more weeks, she was able to go home to raise the little boy with her husband, who she loved dearly. Do you want to know who the man and child were?"

"Yes. And you'd better not be telling me a tale. You know that I can look it up as well." He promised her that it was the truth, as far as he could find. "Then who were they?"

"Devlin Sawyer and his son." He watched her face. He'd do anything to give her a smile and a laugh, but right now he wanted to know that she loved the story behind the gift. "Devlin passed away some years ago. But the son, he's still around, and I called him about it when I found the information about the bracelet. He told me that he'd sold it for his son to go to college. They'd run into hard times after his father had passed on, but his grandson, have you guessed who it is?"

"The doctor. Our doctor. Todd is his son." He nodded at her and was glad for her smile. "I'm betting that you offered to give it back to the man, didn't you?"

"I did, but he turned me down. Told me that I should give it to someone that I love as much as he did his family. I told him all about the love of my life, and he said that he'd be glad to know that someone was wearing it that would appreciate the work that had gone into it. He said that his dad hadn't taken it out of the box since the day that his biological mother had taken off. And when his wife passed away, he'd simply not wanted anything to do with it." TJ looked at it on her wrist and was glad for the way it fit her. "I made him a promise that day. He told me not to tell his grandson. It's better that he goes on thinking that his grandma is the woman that Devlin's son called Mom. He sure

87

thought of her as his momma, he told me."

"What a wonderful gift, and a lovely story." She looked at the bracelet that had been custom made for the man. There were nine wolves, all in a line separated by diamonds. And the clasp was a paw that had a large sapphire in the middle of it. The blue of it matched the dress that Christine had on.

TJ was proud to have his family here with him for this. Sterl had gone through some rough times of late, and he was happy too that he'd found his mate. Marty was a stickler for things, all right, but she sure did keep Sterl on his toes. He was going to enjoy watching her come to her own.

As soon as they stepped off the elevator, he saw them. All his sons were tall, big men that worked and played hard. And he loved them more than he thought he could ever put into words. There were times that he'd regretted being immortal, but today, especially right now, he was happier than if he'd invented it all by himself. He was going to see so much and live so well through the grandchildren coming to these sons of his.

Trent was standing tall next to his lovely Joe. Elijah was holding Noelle's hand and rubbing her back. They were going to make them grandparents soon, and TJ was head over heels in love with that idea. Scott was as happy as he'd ever seen the boy. His bride was the chief of police and they were having a real set down, something his dad would say about getting things in order.

His dad and mom came to stand with them as they gathered around, and TJ realized then how much he loved his parents. He'd always known of course, but it was hitting him hard that he'd have them forever now. Hugging his dad, then his mom, he grabbed his dad again and told him how happy he was to be around now.

"I am too. I surely am. I never thought that I'd be prouder of them grandboys than when they called me Grandda for the first time. But here we are about to embark on a career that will make them shine. Yes, sirree. I'm about as glad as I've ever been that I'm still kicking."

Sterl was with Marty, and he had to blink twice when he saw what she was wearing. The girl looked like she'd been dressed in the finest of silks and knew just how pretty she looked. However, Sterl was a little pale, even stiff. He couldn't blame him, this was going to be a big deal for him.

Going to his son, he put out his hand and shook Sterl's. "This is going to put your name on charts like you've never seen." If possible, TJ thought his son paled a little more. "You're going to be just fine, son. You can count on it."

"Marty said the same thing. I'm sick over this." He could see that. Sterl had been through some rough times, but he was actually holding up better than he thought he'd be. "Dad, I think I'd like to go home now."

"Now you see here, I got myself all gussied up for this, and you're going to go too. Why, how you gonna hear them people talking about how talented you are if you're not there?" He said it wouldn't be praise but something far worse. "You leave those naysayers to me. I'll make sure that they're on the right path of seeing the best painter of all times. I don't think it's going to be a problem, mind you, but I'll have a talk with them if they do."

"Dad, you've never even seen these paintings. For all you know they could really be crap." TJ said he refused to believe that. "I'm painting what I saw that night and the nights that followed. It was pretty horrific."

"I'm betting that it was. And I'm right sorry that I wasn't able to help you with that woman. But you're getting better all the time. You have yourself a lovely mate that loves you, and in a few years, less I hope, you'll have your own son or daughter to bounce on your knee and you'll not think of that time at all." Sterl didn't look like he believed him. "You will never forget, Sterl, but you can move on from it."

The limos that had been arranged to pick them up arrived. He was riding with Sterl and Marty, along with his own mate and parents. They were quiet on the ride over, but he was sure it was due to the tension in the car. He'd be all right, TJ thought, once people started coming in and talking about the art. TJ couldn't wait to see it for himself.

~~~

Isaac wandered around the gallery. There were several people that he knew, a few he didn't. But he could certainly recognize the Calhouns. They were all standouts when it came to good looks, and they were tall too. Christ, he'd hate to have to tangle with any of them. But he liked them, very much so, and he loved their mates. Marty was the best of all, he thought, with the way she kept talking poor Sterling down from his panic attacks. He almost hated to bring up the new development.

"Sterling? If I may have a word—" Sterl started shaking his head before he got to finish. "I swear to you, you'll want to hear this."

"No, I can't see how I can. You want to close the gallery, right? You just realized what a fraud I am. I don't blame you. I've tried to—" His grandmother hit him in the back of the head. "I'm just trying to soften the blow."

"There is no blow if you don't listen to the man. Now, hush and let him tell you." They all looked at him and Isaac had the most insane need to laugh. "Go on, Isaac. Tell us what you came here to say."

"There's an offer on the one called Redemption. I have asked, and if you agree to sell it, he'll gladly leave it here for the showing. Also, Death has an offer as well, but I'm holding out for the show. I told the man that we wanted to see how it went." Sterling looked at Marty then back at him. "What would you like to do?"

"I don't have a clue." Isaac laughed and thought this man was going to be his greatest artist as well as a dear friend. "You said they're willing to hold off taking it? Then I'm okay with that, I guess. Have they really looked at it? I mean, they've seen it up close?"

"Yes. He's still here if you'd like to be assured that he has seen it. He was quite taken with it." Sterling didn't move. "He has no idea that you're here, if that's what is worrying you."

"Yes, I mean no." He looked at his family before speaking again. "I'm going to take my family around, and if he's still in there, I'll think about talking to him. But I'm sure that whatever you think is right, then I trust you."

It occurred to Isaac as he was walking away that he'd not asked the price. Sterling was going to be in for a big surprise when he finally got around to telling him. He approached Mr. Millview and waited for the man to wipe his face. He'd been crying when he'd left him moments ago.

"He said that if you would be willing to wait until after the showing, he'd sell it. I do have another interested party on Death." He nodded and told him he'd pay him as soon as his man got here. "Thank you. You're getting a good piece, Mr. Millview."

"Yes, I think I am as well. So much emotion in this one. All of them, really. But this one, it speaks to me on so many levels. I'd surely like to speak to the artist, but I can understand his need for privacy." They both looked at the couple coming in the room. Mr. Millview nodded but turned back to look at the painting. "This is by far the best piece of work I've ever witnessed. And you know me, I'm a collector. You put me down for Death too. I think I need that one as well. It's a beautiful piece. Whatever the asking price is, add me in at another grand, and if the other person goes higher, let me know."

Just as he was about to tell him that he'd do that, Marty, dragging Sterling with her, went up to the man. She simply smiled at him and then introduced themselves. The look on Mr. Millview's face was priceless, and one that he'd not forget for a long time.

"Hello. My name is Marty Hamilton, soon to be Calhoun." Mr. Millview shook her hand and congratulated her. "Thank you. This is the man I'm marrying, Sterling Calhoun. He's the artist."

His face went from happiness to disbelief in seconds. Mr. Millview had been a patron of the gallery since before Issac's dad had left it to him. And now Millview was a regular for him as well. But to see him with an artist that he was admiring, Isaac was glad to have been there to witness it.

"You did this?" Sterling nodded. "My goodness, young man. I do hope you've recovered from this tragedy. It looks like you were put through hell with this."

"I did, and I'm getting there, especially with the help of these works." They both turned and looked at the painting. "This was at my darkest time. I wanted to be sure that you knew what you were getting."

"Yes, I do. I can see sorrow here, and death. The things that I see here are powerful. Completely breathtaking in their horror, as well as beauty. And now that I've met you, I can see more of the progress in the other paintings as well. You did well, young man. Very well indeed. You've gone through this and come out on top. And I've no doubt that you've survived because you needed to. And I'm betting a swift kick to the ass end from the family too."

"Yes, you have that right. My family sort of bullied me into coming out on top."

They both laughed and Isaac stepped away. He needed a moment to gather himself, and he thought that whatever happened from now on, Sterling and Mr. Millview would be better for it.

As soon as he stepped into the back room, he was hit hard from behind and felt his head split open. But he didn't lose consciousness, so when he was rolled to his side, he could see that his brother had come in sometime in the last hour.

"What are you doing here? Robert, you were told that you weren't to gain entrance to this place." Robert told him he shouldn't have done that. "Well, after what you did to those crates, I don't know why you'd expect anything different. What were you thinking?"

"That you owed me money, and that you lied to me." He asked him about what. "You said that I could come in and work with you. You never told me that if I didn't, I'd not be getting paid. I think that's a sort of crucial point, don't you? I want you to stop this nonsense right now and give me whatever cash you have on you, and then I'll think about not killing you."

"No one expects to get paid for not working, Robert. I'm pretty sure you knew that all along." His head was hurting badly now and he was sick from it. "What do you think is going to happen now that you're in here? There are guards all over the place. You won't get away with this."

"I already have. I just want you to give me money. More than you were paying me too. I have decided that you can afford it. And if you don't, then I don't care about that either. I should have been paid all along without all these stipulations that you put on it. Work is for dummies, and I most assuredly am not dumb. What do you think I did that was so terrible that you had to cut off my pay?" He told him. "So? They were well paid for fucking me on the clock. You should be happy that I didn't kill them too. I have, you know. Killed the women I fucked so that they'd not be demanding money from me. And who gives a shit if I was sleeping too? Do you have any idea how exhausting it is to be me?"

His brother was insane. Or he was giving a very good imitation of it. To think that he thought that just because it was something that he wanted that Isaac should simply give it to him

93

KATHI S. BARTON

was nuts. And he told him that.

"Your opinion doesn't matter to me. And I'm not insane. I'm just a man that is used to getting what he wants when he wants it. And you, my dear brother, have been fucking with that. Now, where can you get money for me? You've changed the locks so I can't get into the office where the safe is. I'm guessing that even if I could, you've fixed that to suit you as well, correct?" Isaac told him that he didn't have money here. "Yes, you do. I know you do. How else do you take the money for those stupid artists? You just let them write you a check? I don't think so. Give me some money, Isaac, so that I can get out of here."

"I have about fifty on me. I can give you that if you promise to never return." Robert just laughed. "I don't have any more than that. I swear. I'll give it to you and you can just go about your business and I will mine. I'm not going to pay you either. You're stupid if you think that I will. Especially after what you've done to me and this place."

"No. Damn it, Isaac. This is not going to bode well for you. I told you, I need money. Fifty dollars wouldn't even buy me a dinner out. Get your ass to your office and get me something more. Don't hold out on me, Isaac, I'm your brother." He kept saying that like it was supposed to be special. Well, he was his brother too. And when he pointed that out to him, Robert laughed.

"Why do you find that to be funny? We're brothers, and I'm sure that brothers do not demand money from each other, and they certainly don't hit them over the head with something. What did you hit me with?" He showed him and Isaac felt his fear double. "That was mine from my home."

"Yes, I know. That's where I was before coming here, and your wife didn't have shit either. Not in the form of money anyway. You should take better care of your things, Isaac. They might come up ruined or missing." He was ready to beg him to

94

tell him what had happened, but a noise on the other side of the door alerted them that someone was coming. "I'll be back. And when I am, you'd better fucking have my money."

Then he was gone. Isaac pulled out his phone, calling his home. And when the call went unanswered, he panicked. He'd hurt them. Isaac was sure that his brother had harmed his family. Going into the hallway, he found the courier talking to Millview. Turning right, he went to find one of the other Calhouns. He needed their help right now.

"My wife." He was out of breath, his head pounding, but he tried again to tell Trent what he needed. "My wife was at home with our son. Robert was just here, and I think he might have hurt them. Please, I can't get in touch with her, and I need to know that she's all right."

"I have men at your home. I'll contact them now." He didn't tell him he was being silly. That his brother would never do anything to them. "There are nine men at the house. We're going to go into your office and take care of this."

"Yes, please. I don't want to spoil things for Sterling if this is nothing more than my brother being an ass." Trent nearly carried him to his office. His head was pounding now, his legs feeling less than stable too. After having his brother call for a doctor, Trent closed the door behind him. "He was here. He was in the storage room and he hit me with a bat that my wife kept at the doorway at our house. Have you gotten in touch with any of them yet?"

"Yes, they're going in the house. Two of my men aren't answering me." This was going to be bad, he knew it. Robert had killed Trent's men and his family too. He had no idea why he thought that, but he just knew that's what he'd done. "They're in the house, Isaac. There is blood in the kitchen."

"Oh Christ." When Trent sat down in the chair across from him, he knew. "Where is she? Did he...? Did she suffer much?"

"She's...I'm so sorry, Isaac. Your wife has been murdered.

95

And I think she might have suffered badly. I'm sorry, so very sorry. Peter said that he hears your son. He's.... They have him. They found him in the bottom of a chest of drawers. They said that he's unharmed." Isaac felt his belly churn up and his head spin. Before he could make any kind of comment, he felt himself simply fall over. Then nothing else.

CHAPTER 8

Robert wasn't sure what the big deal was. It's not like he'd gone to his brother's house to kill anyone. Premeditated murder could get you into a lot of trouble. He knew this. But, had she just done what he wanted then things would have been so much easier on her. And now because of her stupidity, he was a wanted man.

His picture was plastered all over the news. They were even putting it under programs that were running too...his face, and that he was armed and dangerous. That wasn't right. He had no guns, just the baseball bat that he'd taken from the house. None of this was making any sense to him. It was all on Isaac, and no one was saying a word about how he'd lost his job because of his brother.

Then there was Isaac. He had no idea how he thought that he could just fire him. It wasn't as if he'd done anything to warrant it. Of course, he supposed that he could have not taken the whores into the building. But if he hadn't, then he'd have had to pay them to drive to where he was staying. His way, he'd saved nearly two hundred dollars a pop by having them just come to where he was working. If anything, Isaac should be proud of him for being so thrifty. But instead he had fired him, and had him dragged from the building like he wasn't anything or anyone important.

Now here he was, sitting in an abandoned building with nothing to entertain him. He wasn't even able to use his phone for fear of someone tracking it. He looked over at it when it buzzed. It was Isaac again, his picture taking up all the screen like he was so important.

Robert tried to think how long he could stay on the phone before someone could track him. He was sure it was less than five minutes, but he wasn't positive. But it was getting on his last nerve that Isaac thought he was so stupid that he'd allow him to let the police find him.

Finally, when it stopped ringing, he looked around where he was. The dead man in the corner bothered him a bit. It was as if he were accusing him of something that he'd done. Another thing to blame on his brother and sister-in-law was this man's death. Had he only just left the building when Robert had asked him to then he'd be living the rest of his filthy life out normally. Poor, of course, but he'd be alive.

The phone rang again and he nearly tossed it across the room when he noticed that the call was from an unknown number. Picking it up, he answered without saying a word.

"Come now, you don't want me to think that you don't care for me, do you?" He knew the voice but wasn't sure. "You called me the other day and warned me about putting my things in the gallery. Well, warned is a tame word for it. I believe you threatened me, then tried to bribe me. Isn't that right?"

"Calhoun?" The caller laughed. "I don't think I caught your first name. I just got a glimpse of the contact on my brother's desk, but not really a name. Why are you calling me now? Surely you've seen what Isaac has done to me."

"I have, yes. But I think you're wrong about what he's done to you, and it's more what you've done to him. As for my name, no, I suppose you'd not have it, now would you? The thing is, you hurt a very dear friend of mine. Poor Gloria didn't stand a chance with you beating her to death with a ball bat, now did she? And that poor baby. You—"

"I did nothing to that brat. I couldn't find it no matter how much I looked. You can bet that I'd have not left it around either, had I found that little cocksucker." There wasn't any kind of response, so he continued. "You didn't really think that I'd not hedge my bets, did you? I mean, if he should die, then he does. My father should never have left him that place anyway. I'm only younger than Isaac by ten minutes. But that's not fair to penalize me for not being first and getting everything I wanted. Don't you think?"

"You would have run it into the ground and we both know it. I think your father was a smart man to have left it to the smarter of the two of you, regardless of who was born first." He started to tell her he was the smarter when she continued with a hearty laugh. "In fact, now that you'll be in prison for a very long time, if not on death row, then I'd say he really did the smartest thing by not leaving it to you."

It occurred to him that she could be recording this. Or even tracking him. But he knew artist types to be vain and sort of stupid. Especially ones that would stoop to coming to the Sullivan Gallery. No, she'd not be smart enough to do something like that.

"You should know something, Calhoun. As soon as I can arrange it, I'm going to go after that brat, and even my brother. No one will be able to stop me either." She asked him why not. "Because I'm going to say it was insanity from being fired from my job, as well as it being my family thing. No court in the land will convict a man that has had everything taken from him."

"So, you're going to say that being fired made you insane?" He told her of course. "Well, I'm not sure, but I think people thought you were insane well before you were fired, Bobby. The very idea that you think that is going to fly is just ludicrous. Don't you think?"

99

"I'm not Bobby. My mother named me Robert. And no, I don't think it's ludicrous. I think it's brilliant. Isaac was always the stupid one in our family. Why he ever hired me in the first place is beyond me. Even if Mommy would have told me to, I'd have never hired me. But now that he has, he should have made it so that I could draw a check there forever. And firing me? That shit will never happen again either."

"Of course not. If you think you're in charge, I can see where you'd not fire yourself." He wasn't sure what she meant, but laughed when she did. "Well, this has been fun, but I've done all I can do today. Thanks."

"For what? Are you going to help me out?" She told him that she already had. "How? I didn't hear you say you were going to let me sell your paintings."

"No, I didn't. And that's not going to happen at all." She laughed and his temper hurt his head. "By the way, you're surrounded."

He heard the sirens then. Standing up with the phone still in his hand, he looked out the window and down the street. He was indeed surrounded, but he wasn't sure what all the fuss was about. He'd killed his sister-in-law in self-defense. It wasn't as if she were alive to say anything different. So instead of running, he decided to play the insane card to the fullest.

When the police came into his little area of the building, he was taken to the floor and his hands cuffed behind him. He didn't say a word. Robert was afraid that they'd hear intellect in his voice and his insanity plea would be over. Watching them, he forgot about the dead man in the corner and only shrugged when asked about him.

"Robert Conrad Sullivan, you're under arrest for the murder of Gloria Sullivan, William Luna, Jacob Smithy, and the attempted murder of Isaac Sullivan—"

"What does that mean, attempted? I did nothing of the sort.

And if you think I killed my poor sister-in-law, I'm going to tell you right now, it was her fault. She came at me first. And I have no idea who those other two are. You're adding names just to make things sound worse for me. I won't have it, I tell you." The officer just looked at him with that "sure she did" look. And explained to him that the others were the guards around the house he'd murdered when he'd gone into the house. "Oh. Well, they were in the way. But I swear, she had this bat there, and as soon as I got in the house, she hit me with it."

"Got in the house? You mean, when you forced your way in." Robert told him how she wouldn't open the door. "So, you admit to breaking into your brother's home and killing his wife?"

"I didn't kill her on purpose." He asked him why he'd done it in the first place. "She was supposed to give me money. And when she said she didn't have any, I asked for my niece. Or nephew. I can't remember. But I was only going to hold him until my brother hired me back and then paid me. I know that he can't just pay me without hiring me, so I asked, nicely mind you, for her to give me the brat so that I could have something to bargain with when I talked to Isaac again."

"You are aware that it's kidnapping, aren't you?" He said it was a relative, so it didn't count. "Yes, it does. When you take someone against their will or their caretaker's, then that's kidnapping. You just admitted to wanting to take the child for gain. That's kidnapping almost word for word in the dictionary."

Robert didn't think he had that right but said nothing. As soon as he was home again, he was going to look it up. Robert had done a lot of research on things before going to Isaac's house. And he was as up on the laws as these bozos were. Probably more so.

As the officer finished reading him his rights, Robert tried to think who he needed to contact with his one phone call. His brother was the only person he knew. There was a lawyer too, but for the life of him he couldn't think of his name. But he was sure that Isaac would remember it and call for him. There wasn't any way that Isaac would leave him in jail for more than a couple of hours.

He was taken to the jail in one of the larger vans. It wasn't as nice as the car might have been. First of all, there were four armed men in the back with him, and they were rude, not answering a single question of his, nor wanting to joke around. The second thing that was pissing him off, there wasn't any way for him to hold onto the seat. He wasn't buckled in, and every time they went around a curve too sharply, he'd fall over. Finally, he just laid on the floor rather than get up to be knocked down again. And the assholes with him thought it was funny.

When he was brought into the jail the back way, he noticed the television crews. There were several local, as well as a few statewide, ones. He thought he saw someone from the newspaper too and asked about it. He didn't expect a response, and was surprised when one of the men answered.

"They're here for a murderer. When a person kills someone and even admits to trying to kill a child as well, people get up in arms. Go figure." He wasn't sure who they were talking about and asked. "You. You are the one that they're pissed at. I think that they're justified in it, but that's just me."

"I didn't admit to anything." He thought about the conversation with Calhoun. "I can't be recorded unless they tell me about it. I know my rights."

"So, you admit to telling her that you killed Gloria while Calhoun was recording you?" Robert nodded. "You're telling me that you admitted to killing Gloria Sullivan, your sister-in-law, when talking with Calhoun on the phone earlier? And those two men?"

"Yes, of course. But she can't use that against me. I wasn't informed that I was being recorded." He asked him if that counted body cams. "I would guess not. They're supposed to keep the people safe, aren't they? It's not as if you did anything to me that I'd have to call you out on. But that stuff with that artist person, she said nothing about recording me. By the way, how did you find me? She didn't strike me as smart enough to do some kind of GPS on me."

"She's very smart, Especially since the chief was telling her what to say to you. Keeping you on the line was a good deal easier than any of us thought it would be." Damn it, Robert thought. Was no one honest anymore? "Now, you just go on into the cell here and we'll get this cleared up."

"I should hope so. I have things to do today, and none of it will get done with me behind bars." When the officer walked away, he realized that he'd forgotten to ask about his one call. Well, he'd get it next time. Anyway, the officer had already told him that he was working to get this cleared up. Soon, he'd be out and looking for his brother to take care of things.

The cell he was in was bare. There was a cot, yes, and a commode that he was sure was meant as a scare tactic. There wasn't any way that he was going to be able to use that thing without a curtain or something. The blanket at the end of the bed was soft but not overly large. Nor was it very thick. He'd have to see about getting someone to get him an electric blanket if he ended up spending the night for some reason. Robert didn't like being cold at night.

As the time ticked by, he was beginning to worry that they'd forgotten about him. Just as the sun was going down, he realized he was hungry. Standing up when he heard the door opening at the end of the hall, he saw someone coming toward him with a tray. Finally, someone to give him some much-needed answers. At the last second, he remembered he was supposed to be insane.

"I'd like to call my brother, please. Also, if you could please tell me why I'm in here, I'd very much appreciate it." His tray was slid under the bars and the man started to walk away. "Hello? Did you hear me? I need to call Isaac. I can't remember the name of our family attorney. I need someone to come here and get me out."

The man paused and turned to look at him. He didn't say anything but stood there, so Robert tried again to get him to understand what was happening. Also, he asked about the blanket.

"This isn't a hotel, you know that, don't you?" Robert said that it barely passed for a cell. "It's the minimum that we have to provide. There won't be any calls yet as the phone system that you can use is out of order. Also, I'm not thinking you're going to get an electric blanket of any kind. I can bring you an extra one of those should you want it, but nothing electric. We don't want you to have any sort of accident while under our care."

The man left him there, and it wasn't until Robert was sure he wasn't returning that he looked at his meal. This was ridiculous. Ham on whole wheat bread? No, it should have been rye, everyone knew that. And a bag of carrot sticks as well as some sort of dip. There were also two things of milk and an apple. This was a diet meal, and he was far from fat.

~~~

Sterl walked into the living room to see Joe holding the Sullivan baby in front of her. Her arms were stretched out and the little guy was hanging from her hands. Joe was holding him under his arms about a foot from her body. It looked to him like they were having a staring contest and the child was winning.

"Whatcha doing?" She told him that she'd been asked to watch the infant. "I see. You do know that you don't have to watch his every movement, don't you?"

"When I tried to lay it down, it cried." He told her his name was Benson. "Yes, Benson. When I tried to put him down, he cried. He doesn't when he's like this."

"How long have you been holding him out like that? I mean, you look like you're not enjoying having a baby in your arms." He laughed when she growled at him. "Seriously, why are you not holding him in your lap?"

"I told you, it cries." He told her again it was Benson. "I know his name, damn it. I just don't want it to cry again. It makes my whole body hurt to hear it."

"Do you want me to help you?" She looked at him with pleading eyes. "Joe, you have to set him down for a moment. He has had some tragic things happen to him in the last few days."

"You think he misses his mom?" Sterl told her that he was sure that he did. "Sterl, if you could please take him from me and not let him cry, I'd really appreciate it. When they asked me to keep an eye on him, he was sleeping, but that didn't last very long. In seconds—I'm betting they weren't even at the car yet—he was awake and bawling like he was going to break the sound barrier."

He took the baby from her and sat down on the chair. Benson was a cute little guy. Fat cheeks and pretty blue eyes. Sterl took his hat off, and the little boy smiled at him then looked over at Joe.

"I don't think he trusts me." Sterl asked her why she'd think that. "I don't know. It's the way he looks at me. Like he's waiting for me to mess up or something."

"I doubt very much that he's learned how to distrust someone yet. He seems to be just fine. Want to hold him again?" She shot off the couch like a starter pistol had gone off and she was in the lead. "Why on earth did you offer to watch him if you're so afraid of him?"

"Isaac said that he needed to go to the bank, and he asked if Trent would take him. I think he needed to get away for a few hours. And he's making funeral arrangements this afternoon too." Sterl told her how they'd caught Robert. "Yes, we heard.

105

Marty called here right after she got off the phone with him. She told me what Robert said to her."

Sterl had heard as well, and it chilled him to his very core to know that the man was that heartless. Benson cooed a little and grabbed his tie. Looking at the clock over the mantel, he asked when the baby had eaten last. Since it had been a few hours, he took him to the kitchen to find something for him to eat. Sterl thought of the things that he and Marty had talked about this morning.

The showing was going to proceed as scheduled. Sterl was also going to be the artist in the house. Mr. Millview had convinced him of that last night at the premiere by giving him the confidence that he rarely had anymore. They were also going to not worry about the showing, how much things were going for, nor whether or not they'd sell. One thing at a time, they'd decided. He looked at Alta when she handed him some cooked carrots and applesauce.

"There's a high chair in the pantry if you'd like to use it." Before he could hand her the baby and get it, she was bringing it out to him. "I'm thinking that this little man feeds himself all right, but you might need to help him a little. He'll be a mess after."

"I don't mind." He didn't either. Sterl had been a teacher before the accident, and he loved kids. Not as much as his brother Randal did, but he had enjoyed them. "I was thinking that I might need to make some arrangements about tonight. I know that Isaac said it was all taken care of, but I worry about him. I don't know what I'd do if something ever happened to Marty."

"You'll be just fine and I've talked to the little woman that is running the place for Isaac tonight. She said that the caterers have been called in, as well as waiters and waitresses. I've a few of my own there, just in case. Also, you should know that the Bentleys are going to be there, in full force. You can't get any

106

better than that when it comes to protecting you. You all will be fine and dandy."

Sterl nodded and fed Benson. He was able to feed himself, but he was using his hands more than the spoon. And a lot of it was ending up in his hair as well as on Sterl. Every time Benson slapped his hands on the tray and Sterl jumped, Benson would laugh like he'd been tickled.

He liked the Bentleys. They were cougars, and an assortment of other creatures as well. In addition to a witch, the grand witch at that, there was another shifter, a faerie, as well as a couple that he didn't know that well yet. Sterl was glad that someone was going to be watching their backs while he humiliated himself in front of a group of people. Laughing to himself, he finished lunch with Benson.

He fed the baby the applesauce, then he gave him some round cereal that he enjoyed watching the little guy pick up and eat while he enjoyed a sandwich of his own. Benson had a sippy cup and was using that, but he would need a bottle when naptime came. And as he was falling asleep while he was eating, Sterl thought it was about that time anyway.

Taking the little boy to the living room, Sterl smiled up at Marty when she joined him there. Rocking Benson and talking to her in low tones, he told her where Isaac had gone. He also told her about Joe and the baby.

"Yes, I don't think she's the cuddle type. I can see her doing that. Holding the baby so still so as not to upset him." They both laughed. "I was so afraid that Robert would figure out what we were doing. I know that Chloe said it would be fine, but I was still worried. And I feel bad that he thinks I'm the artist."

"I don't care, love. I'm just glad this guy is behind bars and he can be out of our lives forever. I do worry about Isaac, but I think with support he'll be all right." She said that she hoped so, he was a good man. "He really is. I just hope that he and Benson come out on top of this. Like you, I worry about him too."

Alta and her niece, another witch, were going to watch the little boy and protect him when they went out. He wasn't sure where Isaac was going to be, but here or there, he'd be in good hands. Sterl hoped things turned out well for them all.

The opening was at five, and at four o'clock he joined Marty in their room to dress. Violet had shown up and taken over the care of Benson, as Isaac was running behind. But Benson seemed to like her, so it was all right with Sterl to leave them together.

"I need your help with my zipper." Sterl nearly swallowed his tongue when Marty presented her back to him. When she turned to ask him what was wrong, he nodded and pulled the little tab to the top. Really, what he wanted to do was take the dress off her, but he knew they'd be late. And he'd been warned by both his grandparents and parents not to let that happen. "I'm not sure that this is going to be a good dress to wear tonight."

When he got his tongue working again, he smiled at her. "I think this dress would be much prettier on the floor beside our bed, but we have to leave on time. I think the limo is going to be here in fifteen minutes."

"We could fool around in the car." He shook his head and told her he'd been warned about that as well. "Well, I don't know how they expect us to make them grandparents if they have all these rules to follow."

"You want children?" He pulled on his tux after stripping down. "We never talked about it. I do. Lots of them, if you want to."

"I do, and soon." She bent at the waist to get her shoes and he wanted to bite her. Marty caught him looking at her ass. "If you keep that up, not only will we be late, but we might not make it at all."

While he was completely all right with that, he did agree to behave, but he couldn't help himself, so Sterl did keep looking at her body. And damn, but she had a fine one too.

CHAPTER 9

"I would like to have you notarize something for me." The bank manager said he'd do anything for him, and gave him his condolences as well. "Thank you. I don't know what I'm going to do without her in my life."

Isaac looked over at Trent as he sat in the little lobby area. Isaac had asked him to bring him here, but had not explained. It was something that he felt strongly about, and he couldn't think of a better family to make it work. Isaac looked at the banker again.

"I'm sure you've heard about my wife and brother." He nodded. "I'm sorry. I've completely lost the memory of your name. I know I should know it, but I've been under so much stress of late."

"That's all right, Isaac. My name is Gavin Music. Your family and mine go to church together as well." He nodded and apologized again. "No need for that. I can't even imagine how much you're going through right now."

"Yes. I'm afraid that it's not over yet, either. I want to...I would like for you to witness and notarize a letter I've written. It's a will of sorts. You have an attorney on staff, correct?" He nodded and told him he'd help. "I don't want anyone to know what I've written here until.... My brother, he's very slick. I worry that he'll be able to get free, and I want to make sure my wishes are seen to. Not only for my gallery, but everything."

"Yes, of course. I can help you with that. Just show me what you want done." He handed him the letter of sorts that he'd written out. Gavin looked up at him once or twice but didn't comment. "I can help you with this, Isaac. No worries there."

"You think it's the right thing to do?" He told him it was the perfect thing to do. "I'm so happy to hear you say that. I've worried, you know. And with my insurance, it should help with any bills I might leave behind. I thank you for this."

They went through the paperwork that would change his will. There was a great deal for him to have to disperse too. After a few more minutes, he was able to withdraw enough money to take care of any business that might happen at the gallery tonight. He wasn't worried about Sterling not making any sales. The man was going to be huge after this evening.

Trent took him to the printer next. This morning he'd learned from Sterling that he was going to tell people he was the artist. It had taken him no time at all to come up with a nice picture of the man to add to fliers, and once he had, the printing company was more than glad to add it. He showed them to Trent and asked his opinion.

"They're wonderful. I can't believe that art you have there, it's from him. I mean, we all knew he was talented, but to see them there, it was mind-blowing." Isaac was feeling human again and told him that he'd been surprised by it as well. "He took a few art lessons when he was a kid. When there was an art show at the school, he'd win that hands down. But to see this, work from his soul, it makes me want to find him and give him a hug. Not to mention, kill that woman again."

"When Jasmine called me about them, I would have taken the paintings just because she'd asked so nicely. Your family and mine have been friends for more years than I could tell you. But once I saw them, the few that he brought me, I must tell you, I was so excited I wanted to buy them myself. Sterling is that good." Trent looked like a proud brother, and he was sure that he was. "Sterling is going to be quite famous after this, if not already. Mr. Millview has a great many influential friends, and he will open the door for him in a great many places that I could only hope for him."

"I knew that he was working some of his stress out by painting. My sister-in-law, Noelle, she took him on a couple of buying trips for antiques with her, and noticed that he had picked up some paints and things. She got him a few canvases, as well as some more supplies, and he was happy. For the first time in a very long time." Isaac said he was very shy about his work. "I think that has more to do with what the story is behind the paintings than the actual art of them. He was in a bad place when that thing came to him. I think, had he had his way, he would have ended his life."

"I'm to understand that you're immortal." He said that the entire family was. "I'm not sure that I'd like that. It might have.... Well, I'm not sure that I would want to go on like this. I know that I have my son, but my wife.... Well, she was everything to me. The reason I'm the man I am."

"I'm sure your wife would have told you to hang around for your son." He nodded and looked out the side window. "We'll all be there for you, Isaac. You know that, don't you? And I'm sure that once things are taken care of, you'll feel better about life. You have a wonderful little boy in Benson."

He was grateful for Trent not telling him that she was in a better place. Or any of the other drivel that people were saying. Like she'd not suffered, or that he was lucky that she'd hidden their son away. He knew that they meant well, all of them, but he was in pain, and their words of comfort seemed so useless to him. His heart was broken, and he didn't think it would ever mend after this.

The ride to the gallery wasn't long, but when they got there, he took a walk around the place to make sure things were just so. He had an assistant that was going to help tonight…Isaac had already decided to be there, but not on the floor. He wasn't sure that he could handle people talking to him any more than he could messing up the showing for a soon-to-be-great artist. Trent walked with him, but didn't comment on the way things were until they were back in the car.

"He's going to shit with those prices." Isaac laughed, the first one in what seemed like years. "I think Sterl has it in his head that they're going to go for a couple of hundred apiece, and a lot less for the smaller ones. You think anyone will want them at those prices?"

"Three of the smaller ones are sold already. Redemption sold as well, but I think we're going to have a bidding war on the one called Death. Honestly, I don't think he's going to have any trouble selling out tonight, or any other showing he has. He's that good." Trent nodded. "He told me that he has a lot of ideas, nightmarish ideas, for a few more paintings, and I told him I'd take them for him. I'm betting by the middle of next year, if not sooner, he's going to be making arrangements to go around the world with his art."

"I know that since meeting Marty, he's been sleeping better. Not perfectly, he told me, but well enough to function now." Isaac said he liked her as well. "So does my family. Even my grandma thinks she's a hoot. All of the women in this family are so grateful for having Sterl almost back to normal, and we have Marty to thank for a great deal of that. I think she's been good for all of us. I know that Noelle and her have become best friends. Not that they exclude Joe or Chloe, but I think the two of them have a great deal more in common."

"Yes, I can see that. Noelle, however, is fragile, while Marty is harder, more to the point. Perhaps you might find a shift in their personalities a little. Where they begin to take on more of the other." Trent said he thought that would be good as well. "I think so as well. You're all, the entire pack of you, good people."

The gallery was as ready as it would ever be. Going back out to the car, he asked if they could make one more stop. That he wanted to go and see his brother. Just once. Trent, of course, said he would be there for him.

The jail wasn't all that busy. He supposed in a town this small they'd have slow days. He knew that Chloe, another Calhoun, had taken over the running of the department when the FBI had come in and made some serious arrests. Anastasia, a warrior fae, had been instrumental in making that happen. And from what he could see and had heard from others, Chloe was doing a great job of it.

"There's a camera on him at all times." He nodded when she briefed him. "Also, don't get close to the doors. He can hurt you if you do. And please don't get into an argument with him. Not for his sake, but for yours. He'll say whatever he wants to in order to make you think he's innocent in all this. Okay? He'll also.... Well, he seems to think that all of this is your fault. It's not...none of us believe that, but he'll say it."

"All right. Yes. Thank you." She nodded and then hugged him. Isaac held her to him tightly, glad for the support. Trent asked if he wanted him to go in with him. "I don't think so. I mean, I might need you there, but I'd like to do this on my own. I will more than likely regret it, but I need this. Closure, I guess."

Making his way down the short hall, he saw his brother. Robert was complaining about something that he couldn't understand, but his anger was palpable. As he approached the doorway, keeping his distance, he looked at Robert and was amazed at the change in him over such a short time.

His hair was untidy. The orange and green striped jumpsuit

he had on didn't do anything for his appearance. There was an air of stench around him that made Isaac think that he'd not bathed or even washed up since he'd been here. And the food that looked as if it had been tossed against the walls didn't improve anything. It was nasty, from the cell to the man behind bars.

When he finally noticed him, Robert stood up. He was dirtier than Isaac thought. There were scraps of food in his beard, stains down the front of him. And his hands, usually so clean and manicured, looked as if he'd been playing in mud. Isaac decided not to look at them again, not liking where his mind went as to what it might be. Keeping his distance, Isaac asked him how he was faring.

"Like you care. Why haven't you gotten back to me? I've sent you messages through these people here. Or are they not telling you about them." Isaac told him he'd gotten them. "Then why am I still in this cell? Isaac, you must get me out of here. I can't stand this. Four days is quite long enough for you to have figured out that whatever lesson you were trying to make me learn is not going to work."

"Too bad. You've only been here one whole day and half of a second, Robert, not four. And I'm not going to help you other than to watch you during your trial. You killed my wife." Robert rolled his eyes and shook his head. "Why did you do that, Robert? She did nothing to you."

"I want you to at least give me the name of our family attorney. If you're not going to help me, then I want him to do it. I'm pretty sure that you have him on retainer or something." He said that he did but he wasn't going to help. "Why the fuck not? I need a good attorney to get me out of this mess you've put me in."

"*I* put you in? I don't think so, Robert. You did this all on your own. And he can't help you because he's helping me." He asked if he'd been arrested too. "No. He's helping me take you to court for the murder of my wife."

"I don't understand why you get the good attorney. Just find yourself someone else. Or better yet, just drop this whole thing and tell them that you don't want me to go to jail. I'm not suited for jail. Then when I get out, you can hire me back. I know you must do that for tax purposes, but if I don't show up, you can still pay me. That way, there won't be whores in the gallery. Also, I need for you to double my salary. If I can't have the women coming to me there, then I'll have to pay them to come to me at my home. I can't afford that on the little you pay me." Isaac couldn't believe he'd just said that. "Are you listening to me? Perhaps you should be writing this down. I know how you like lists."

"I'm not going to hire you back. Are you insane? I fired you because you brought ladies of the night into my gallery. You stole things from other artists as well as the staff, and you fucking killed my wife. And on top of that, had you found my son, you would have murdered him as well." Robert said that he hadn't killed his son, and that should count for something. "Is that supposed to justify this? That since you couldn't find him, you shouldn't be in trouble for any of it?"

"Yes. Christ, you act like this is the end of the world for you. Have you even noticed where I am? What I'm wearing? I think of the two of us, I'm much worse off. And you should see what they're feeding me. Damn it, Isaac, get me out of here. I have shit to do." Isaac just stared at him. "I need for you to get on the stick, and this time when I'm working for you, I want a contract. That way we won't have to go through this again."

"Are you going to kill me, Robert?" He wasn't sure that he was going to answer him. He stared at him for several seconds before he nodded. "If I were to get you out of here, have the charges dropped, you'd still try your best to kill me."

"Isaac, you have to see that you've brought this all on

117

yourself. I mean, look at what you've put me through. I've been arrested for no reason. Hunted like a common criminal. There are things that I've been accused of that just aren't true." Isaac asked him what that might be. "They're saying that I went to the house to murder your wife. I didn't. I went there to murder you, and get some money. She wouldn't give me your kid so that I could hold him up to make you pay me what I wanted. That officer tried to tell me it was kidnapping, when I know better. The kid is my nephew, not some stranger. They said that I also robbed you. All I took was a few things to tide me over until I killed you."

Isaac had enough. He couldn't stand there and listen to his own flesh and blood justify his actions. And to have his mind so set on things being done for him, without consequences for any of it, was deplorable. As he made his way out of the area, he heard his brother asking him when he was going to be freed. It was all he could do to make it to the bathroom and throw up. Isaac was sickened by it all.

~~~

Sterling was doing great. Marty watched him talk to people about what had driven him to make such wonderful pictures, and they were awed by his candid story about what had inspired him. Several people had gone away shaking their heads, saying that they'd known Sterling all his life and were amazed that so much talent had been hidden. Marty went to him when he had no one to talk to for a moment.

"How you holding up?" She snagged them a plate of goodies when the waiter walked by, and watched him wolf down several before speaking. "I guess you have your appetite back."

"Yes, and I'm doing well, I think. The biggest relief I have is that I've not puked on anyone yet, and I've remembered my name each time I'm asked." He kissed her. "It was touch and go there for a minute when Mr. Garber, my science teacher in high school, asked me if any of the pictures were from my time in his class. It took me just a little too long, I think, in answering him. But he thought it was funny, so all's well now."

"They're all sold." He stopped chewing and gave her a blank look. "Did you hear me? All the paintings are sold. Well, two aren't actually sold yet there's a bidding war for them. Quite a bit too. I never—"

He put his hand over her mouth and told her to hush. Marty couldn't help but grin behind his hand. He was positively green right now. And adorable with the cookie crumbs still on his mouth.

"I don't want to know." She nodded. "Okay, I do want to know, but I don't too. I'm having fun. Knowing this sort of makes me queasy. Just tell me, 'Sterling, you're doing well.' Okay?" He removed his hand slowly, as if he were afraid she was going to tell him more about the bidding war.

"Sterling, you're doing well." He nodded and wrapped his arm around her waist as they made their way to another part of the gallery. "Mr. Millview wants to talk to you, by the way. He said he has a question about one of the paintings."

"He's a nice man." She agreed with him. "I'm worried about Isaac. Did you know that he's here and hasn't left his office since he arriving this evening?"

"I knew he was here, but no, not about the office. Trent said that he went to see his brother this afternoon. I guess it didn't go well." Sterling shook his head. "The poor man. He's lost so much in such a short amount of time. Even though his brother is still alive, in a way he has lost him as well."

They found Mr. Millview, Donald he asked them to call him, and Sterling talked about the painting he was standing in front of. Mercy, the name of this one, was a single painting but larger than most of them. It was of the demon, Richard. Half of Richard was the demon, his tail wrapped around his feet. A single long horn was on the right side of his head. His body was blistered and looking red, and his eyes seemed to be molten hot.

The left side was of a man. A very good looking one. A nice suit, shoes that were covering his hooved feet. He was smiling too, his other eye a blue so clear it looked like he was sightless. And at his feet was the blackened earth, a dagger lying on it. Marty shivered when she thought of what Sterling had gone through during this bleakest part of his life.

She looked at Sterling when he pulled her closer. Marty realized that while lost in the horror of the painting, she'd missed the entire conversation. When she looked at Donald, he winked at her as he continued to speak to Sterling.

"So, we have a deal then? You'll help me out with this?" Sterling squeezed her tighter and she was sure that he was nervous about making a commitment, whatever it might be.

"Yes. I think I can do that. So long as what we agreed on can be accomplished." Donald said that he could do that. "You will talk to Isaac? He's my manager, but I do look forward to hearing from both of you soon."

The two of them shook hands and Sterling pulled her away. When she asked him what was going on, he told her to wait. Just wait. As soon as they were outside, around to the side of the gallery, he pressed her against the wall and kissed her hard.

"He wants me to come to his place of business and paint a mural. Strip for me." He was tearing at her clothing, and she had to smack his hands away so that she'd have something to wear. "Hurry."

"But you'll explain." He nodded and started to pull off his own clothing. "Are you going to be like this every time you get good news? Not that I'm complaining, but you—"

"Marty, I'm trying hard to hold onto my wolf so that he doesn't scare the humans. Take off your clothing and let him have you. You're in heat." It took her befuddled mind several seconds to figure out what he was telling her. "Hurry."

120

She pulled her dress up and over her head, unmindful of the cold. As soon as she was naked, the wolf took him and then her. She cried out when his beast brought her to peak so quickly, and held onto the wall as he made her come over and over. When he licked her thigh, her body tensed up. The bite, like none he'd given her before, brought her over the edge and blurred her vison as well as making her weak.

"I love you." Sterling picked her up, slammed his cock into her, and fucked her hard against the wall. There was no build up, not that any was needed, but she came, screaming out his name and her love for him.

Even as she climaxed numerous times, she needed more. All of him. And when he bit her throat, growling loudly when he did, she came so hard that she fainted from it.

Waking up after what was only seconds, Marty held onto Sterling. He was still breathing hard, his heart pounding too if the pulse at his throat was any indication. When he lifted his head and looked down at her, she fell in love with him all over again. She kissed him gently on the mouth, then laid her head on his shoulder.

"They're going to miss you." He told her that he didn't care. "I don't either, but I thought I should say something. What the hell came over you? Not that I'm complaining, but damn, that was intense."

"I.... You're in heat. I know that I should have talked to you first, but once my wolf realized it, there seemed to be nothing stopping him from taking you." He pulled back enough to look down at her. "Are you all right with having a child this soon? I mean, I'm nearly positive that you are already, but is that okay?"

"Yes, very much so. But I don't want to say anything just yet to your family. I mean, I'd like it to be ours for a while." He laughed and told her that his family would know. "The smell thing, right?"

"Yes, the smell thing. You're so wonderful, Marty. I had no idea what I expected before you came into my life, but I also can't think what it would have been like had you not come along and made me whole again." He kissed her once more, then helped her stand on her own two feet. "I've been meaning to tell you something Alta told me today. In addition to you having this magic, our children will have it as well, and we're marked by the demon so that others of his kind cannot harm us."

"Good to know." She thought of her dress that was now lying in the snow, and wondered what she was going to do now. But instead of worrying about it, she pulled it back over her head and was astonished when it became as lovely as it had been before this. "You think my hair will change too?"

In the end, she simply pulled it back into a ponytail and then twisted it up. It wasn't as beautiful as it had been, but it would pass. They entered the gallery hand in hand and much more relaxed. Trent was waiting for them at the lobby entrance, and she had a feeling that it wasn't to congratulate his brother on a job well done. He looked intense.

"There's a problem." Sterling asked him what it was. "Well, it's about Robert. He just killed a cop that was bringing him dinner and took his gun. They think he's on his way here."

"We need to have someone watching over Isaac." Trent said it was done. "Christ, this guy is really out to fuck up my day. We need to take care of this today, Trent."

"I agree, and we will, once and for all." They made their way into the gallery. Sterl noticed that there were sold signs on all the work as he passed, but for now, he wanted to save his friend. As soon as he entered the office where Isaac had been, he knew immediately that he was gone.

CHAPTER 10

Marty wasn't sure where the other man would have gone. They'd been by his house. The gallery, now closed, had been searched from top to bottom. And she'd even gone to the funeral home that was holding the service for his wife. It was as if Isaac had disappeared right off the face of the earth.

"Have you tried his cell phone?" She nodded at Sterling. "What the hell was he thinking? I mean, there is safety in numbers. We would have been able to protect him."

"Perhaps he didn't want you to protect him." He asked her what she meant. "Well, he's lost his wife and his brother murdered her. Do you suppose that he's just given up?"

"He has Benson." Marty told him that his heart was broken and he was more than likely not seeing it like that. "I can understand that. I felt that way a few times myself. I don't even blame him for it, but I don't want anything to happen to him. He's my friend."

"Mine too. And I don't either. He's a good man that has been dealt a shitty hand. I want him as safe as you do." She wondered if he was with his brother, if Robert had gotten him by luring him away from safety. She didn't want to bring it up because they were all tense enough as it was, but it had to be asked. "Has anyone seen Robert? Or heard from him?"

"No. I hope what we're both thinking hasn't happened. I don't think that Robert will go easy on him whether he agrees to do anything Robert wants or not." That's what she thought as well. "Where do you think he'd take him? If he has him, where is it that he could feel safe enough to do whatever it is he is going to do?"

"The building we found him in? I don't know. Perhaps Robert's home? I don't even know where he lives." Sterling did a U-turn and headed back the way they'd been going. "You know where he is?"

"I think so. Not to Robert's house, but we went by Isaac's. I just asked Trent, and they said they didn't enter because the doors had been watched by the police. So, if Robert can't get in by conventional means, he'll find other ways. Like through the basement doors. I remember Isaac telling me that he had to have it closed off soon before his son started walking." She wanted to ask him to slow down, but felt the same sort of urgency that he was feeling. Like if they didn't hurry, all would be lost.

As soon as they pulled up, Sterling took his cell phone out and called the police. He was telling them where he was and what he was doing when she looked at the officer on the porch. He was in the swing. No biggie, she supposed, until she started up the steps.

"Don't touch anything." Nodding at Sterling who had followed her, she saw it then. The poor officer was dead. His throat had been cut and the knife was still sticking out of his neck. "We've been told to wait. I'm not going to, but you are. This only proves to me that Isaac is going to need help and that his brother is with him."

"Why am I not going in to help you?" He looked at the officer, then back at her. "You told me I was an immortal, and while I'm not a wolf, he's my friend too."

"Yes, he is, but I can shift into a wolf to make myself heal, and you cannot. You are an immortal, but that doesn't keep you from being hurt." She could see his point. Marty didn't like it, but she could see it. "Just go back to the car and wait for the police or me to come out. Please don't enter the house. All right?"

"Yes, I won't. Not unless I hear shots fired or screams, then all bets are off. I know that you can heal, but that doesn't mean my heart will like it any better. Okay?" He kissed her and watched her move to the car. When she told him to be careful, he shifted. He went from man to beast in seconds.

When he shifted back, she thought he'd changed his mind, but all he did was open the door. Sterling as his wolf entered the house and was out of her sight. Marty was terrified something would happen to him and she'd not be able to help.

Just as she was thinking she'd be more help to him closer to the house, Chloe pulled in the drive behind their car. There were other officers as well, but she was the only one that she knew. In her uniform, Marty thought Chloe looked scary. Not that she didn't sort of frighten her a little anyway, but dressed the way that she was, it was official that something really was terribly wrong in the house. Chloe hugged her tightly, then went back to being Miss Cop.

"He didn't wait." It wasn't a question, but she answered her anyway. "I should have known the moment that I said for him to wait that he'd go in. Have you heard from him yet?"

"No. I was just thinking I could hear him better if I went closer to the house, but I'm also afraid of disturbing the crime scene as well." Chloe said they'd have that cleared away next, but first she wanted to go into the house. "Will he be all right?"

"Sterl? Yes. I doubt that Robert will be if something has happened to Isaac. He's a really nice man born to a shitty family." Marty started to ask her what she meant when a howl started. "That would be Sterl. I'm afraid you're going to have to wait here for him. I don't know what's happened, but that doesn't sound

125

good."

It didn't either. It sounded mournful, like he was howling at the moon. Marty felt the hairs on her arm dance along her skin and rubbed the chill from them. It was cold, yes. But this was a deeper chill that had nothing to do with the weather and everything to do with her mate. Marty felt this cold all the way to her bones, right to her very heart.

Trent showed up a few minutes later. By the look in his face, she knew that it was bad. He moved to the house without a word to her, and Joe came to stand beside her. She asked the other woman what was going on.

"They're both dead, Robert and Isaac. I'm so sorry." She asked her if Sterling had done it. "Yes, one of them. He killed Robert. It's not a pretty sight, Trent told me, but Sterl is in a bad way. It's why he can't come out right now. Trent is trying to talk to him, but his mind is a mess."

"Because of the officers here?" Joe told her that he didn't know the police were here yet. "I don't understand. Is he afraid of me?"

"He killed a man. Trent thinks it's the nightmare returning to him with all this. He's covered in blood. It wasn't an easy death for Robert. Nor for Isaac, from what Trent is telling me. He suffered greatly. Again, I'm so sorry. I know he was a very good friend of you both." Marty looked at the house, then back at Joe. "Trent wants me to take you to your home. He said that Sterl is an emotional mess right now and worries for him."

"Fuck that shit. I'm going in there." Joe laughed and told her not to touch anything. "I might do more than touch Sterling. Is that going to be a problem?"

"You might remember someone telling you that you can't hurt your mate, but I don't think that's going to be an issue for you. Go to him and smack his nose. That should get his attention." She wanted more than just his attention, she wanted him to understand that she wasn't a delicate flower he needed to protect. "Marty, he might not know who you are when you first see him. He's in a bad place and seems to not know who anyone is."

"I'll take care of him. I love him." Joe said that they all did. "But he's all I have in this world. I need him well. I just need him to love me."

As soon as she entered the house she could smell the blood. It was overwhelming and made her just a little queasy. Going to the stairwell that led to the basement, she made her way down, careful of not touching the rail nor the walls. On the bottom step, she looked around.

Blood was everywhere, and not just sprayed, but in puddles as well. There was fur as well as torn clothing. In the middle of one particular circle of it was a small shoe. Benson's little sneaker was lying on its side like it might have been left in the rain. Red, nasty rain.

"Marty?" She had to work hard at tearing her eyes away from the scene, then looked at Trent, she could see he had blood on himself as well. When she asked him if he was all right, he nodded to her left, and there she saw Sterling as his wolf. He too was covered in blood, his fur matted with it.

Curled into a ball, he was whimpering. Coming down the last step, she'd started for him when he growled at her. Taking a step back, she glanced at Trent to see what she should do.

"He's not himself. I think.... This is bringing back some of the memories from before. Before you." She nodded and asked if she could touch him. "I'd not do it. He snapped at me. But you might have better luck. Just talk to him, honey. Bring him back to us."

Bring him back from what? she thought. Then it occurred to her. From the paintings that he'd done. That's where he was, she knew, but had no idea how she was supposed to make him come out of the nightmare she was sure that he was having right now.

Walking to him slowly, she started talking to him.

"I'm here for you, Sterling. Forever." His growl made her pause, then he bared his teeth at her. "You're making me think of the little girl and the big bad wolf. Please don't scare me, Sterling. I'm in love with you."

He whimpered again and she got down on her knees. There was blood there, a great deal of it, but she was trying her best to focus only on him. Reaching out her hand, she noticed that it was trembling, but she wasn't going to stop now. Sterling put out his nose to sniff her and whimpered again.

"Joe told me to smack you on the nose. I don't think that would go over too well, do you?" No answer, when she knew he could speak to her as his wolf. "I'm going to have your baby. Remember that? A child of yours and ours to raise and love."

"Marty, try to get closer to him. The police won't come down here until you have him under control." She nodded as Trent spoke to her. "Just be careful. Like I told you, he's not himself."

"I love you, Sterling. I want you to come home with me. We have to...I'm so sorry about Isaac. He was such a nice man." The whimpering again tore at her heart. "Talk to me, Sterling. Please?"

She's here. Marty started to ask Sterling who, but he continued and she understood. *Helenia hurt me. She tried to get me to kill my family. Showed me how to do it in my dreams. It's like she's back here now and talking to me. I hurt, Marty. So badly.*

"If she were still alive, I'd kick her ass from here to the end of time. The fucking cunt." Trent laughed a little, but Sterling laid his head back down. "You have me now, and she's not in your life. I am, and I'm worried about you."

I killed that man. She told him she was glad it was Robert and not him. *I didn't just kill him. I...my wolf, he played with him. Made him suffer. I don't want to be the monster she wanted me to be. I need to go away and not return before I hurt you or our child.*

When he lifted his head up and looked at her, she smacked him hard. When he growled at her, she did it again. This time he stood up and she did as well.

"What are you going to do, Sterling? Kill me because I hit you? Are you going to make me pay for making you feel?" He growled again, and she drew back her hand to hit him a third time. "Do it and I will quit you. I don't mean just leave you, but I will leave you and you'll never see this child, ever. Not only that, but I swear to you, I'll make your life a living hell."

It is now. This time when she smacked him, she saw blood run from his nose. *Damn it, stop hitting me and listen.*

"Why? You're not listening to me. Is it me giving you a horrifying life? Is it our child? Tell me. Tell me how you figure that I'm the one not hurting because of your words." He told her that he loved her. "Do you? I'm not so sure. You just told me that you're living in hell. That does—"

She found herself on her back, Sterling the man, above her. Trent was laughing when she heard him close the door to the basement behind him. Marty looked up at her mate and touched her finger to his nose as it bled a little.

"You hit me." She nodded and smiled at him. "I don't know what happened here. I know that I killed him, but I don't remember much of it."

"You did it because you loved Isaac." He nodded and put his forehead on hers. "I'm in love with you, Sterling, and I hate that you hurt so much."

"I didn't mean that you're giving me a horrific life. But there are times when I can still see what she did to me. What she made me feel." She held him to her. "I can't function when that happens. I'm so afraid."

"Whatever you're doing, wherever you are, you should get up, if you can, and go paint. We'll do whatever you need to go and paint her out of your life. A bigger building. A studio in the house. Anything. Whatever you need." He looked down at her. "I have you, Sterling. I will always have you."

"I hurt so much, Marty. Every day I think of the things that she made me do. How she wanted things from me." She pulled him down for a kiss and was glad that he returned it. "What would I have done without you?"

"You would have been a mess. It's a good thing I'm here to keep you on your toes." She kissed him again. "If it's all the same to you, I'd like to leave this place. It's...I can see blood on the ceiling, and it's making me sort of weirded out."

~~~

They were given clean clothing and theirs was taken away in bags. Sterl wasn't sure what he was supposed to say to anyone, which he supposed was fine since no one was asking him anything. It was like he'd not just been down there and killed a man. Chloe came toward him, dressed in a blue paper suit over her uniform, and smiled.

"You were never here." He nodded. "No, what I mean is, I'd like for you to go home, clean up, and stay there until I call for you. Myra, your friendly witch, has made it so that it looks like a murder-suicide here, and that you were never around. I think I like her, by the way." He told her he did as well. "All right. Go. And while you're at home, I want you to lie down, have a nap, and hold your mate. She's about to bust she's so worried about you."

"She's talking to Joe. I just wanted to have a minute." They both looked at Marty and Joe and noticed that Noah was there as well. "She calmed my beast like no one has ever done before. I think.... He's afraid of her. Did she tell you that she hit me? And that Joe told her to?"

"No, but that's all right, isn't it? I mean, per Trent, you were out of it." Sterl didn't agree or disagree with her, but he had been. "Like I said, this is on the books as a murder-suicide. With all the paperwork we have on Robert, it will be an open and shut case when it hits trial. I'm glad that you didn't wait this time, but the next time I tell you to, please do so. You might not be so lucky next time."

"He is...Isaac was my friend." Chloe said he was a good man and would be missed. "Thank you. I'll head home as soon as Marty is back. I don't want to drive."

They were on their way home when he thought of Benson. Sterl's mom was with him, but the little boy had no idea how much had changed in his young life. Sterl was going to try his best to make things easier for him. Even going to the house again to pick up things from his family. It was the least he could do for the child.

Sterl did just what Chloe told him to do. As soon as he was out of the shower, after scrubbing himself several times, he pulled on his robe. He even tossed the sponge he'd been using into the trash, wanting no more memories of today than he had to have. Entering their bedroom, he saw that the television was off and the lights were dimmed. Removing his robe and crawling into bed with Marty, he held her.

"We have an appointment in the morning with the curator of the gallery. I guess he wants to talk to you about another showing that Isaac had set up for you." He said he'd think about it. "Also, there is someone from the bank that wants to talk to us. I don't know what that one is about."

"I put your name on my accounts. He more than likely wants you to come in and sign the paperwork so that it's completed." He held her closer. "I'm suddenly exhausted. I think I could sleep for a month."

He closed his eyes and let the day's events just move to the back of his mind. He didn't want to think about Isaac nor Robert. His parents still had Benson at their home, but he was going over to see him in the morning, or today he supposed. As he let sleep take him under, he thought of the gallery and wondered who would run it now. Sterling thought for a moment that he might like to buy it if they were going to close.

When he woke, the room was still dim but he thought it was more due to the curtains being closed rather than it being dark out. He felt.... Well, he wasn't sure how he felt, but he wasn't as restless as he had been. Staggering a little to the bathroom, he was surprised to find that it was indeed dark out, and wondered about that as he turned on the water to take another shower. He was just stepping under the spray when Trent started laughing in his mind.

You feel better? He told him he felt wonderful as a matter of fact. *I should hope so. You've been asleep for three days. It was all we could do not to go there and check on your breathing. But Marty said that you were fine and we left you alone.*

Three days? Are you serious? Well, that explained a few things. Like how badly he had to pee. That he was starved and needed another shower. *Have you seen, Marty? I mean, is she all right? I could reach out to her, but I think it freaks her out a little.*

I've noticed that as well. And yes, I just left her with Noelle. They're partners now in the shop. Second Time Around is going to be a big hit, I think. And someone that has information on the desk has come forth too. I think they're going to meet with him in a week. Chloe wants to be there, as well as Chris Bentley. Sterl finished his shower as Trent continued catching him up on things. *Mom and Dad are having fun with Benson. He's staying with them until paperwork is done. Grandma and Grandpa are moving into their own home too. I don't know a lot about it, but they're keeping it all hush hush for now. I could look, but this is more fun for them.*

I'm about to go downstairs. Is there anything I need to know before I do that? Like, is there a squad of cops down there waiting to take me in? Trent said no, not that he knew of. *I killed that man.*

Yes, you did, and thank you for that. And I think had you been in trouble, you wouldn't have rested so well. You must have really needed this. Marty said you were sleeping soundly, like you had not a care in the world. I'm happy for that. He hadn't felt this good in a very long time and told Trent. *You have beaten the demons and it's showing, I think. Not completely yet, but I believe you're on the mend.*

Sterl found that he wanted to paint, and badly. So, he made his way to the kitchen to let Alta know that he was going into town for some supplies. Even as he was making a mental note on things that he wanted, she told him to have a seat and eat, Marty's orders. He sat and reached out for his mate.

Oh, I'm so glad that you're awake. How are you feeling? He told her what he'd said to Trent. *Good. You have some things to take care of when you have time. And so that you know, I had no idea there was so much involved in painting.*

Sterl said that it was sort of an expensive thing. *Why, are you considering taking it up as well? Are you planning on joining me in the world of art?*

No, God no. I was... You haven't looked out back yet, have you? I mean, I figured that you did it, but now I don't know. He stood up and looked out the kitchen window. *It was there that first morning, and I went out to see what it was. Then every time that I stepped in the place, it had more supplies. I had to look a couple of them up. There is a canvas stretcher, numerous rolls of canvas too, and so much paint that I doubt you'd ever have to leave for supplies.*

After eating, he made his way out to the building and opened the door. Sterl was no longer listening to Marty, but just taking in the whole thing. She was right, he'd not have to have supplies brought in for a very long time. And there at the drafting table sat Myra and Chris. He asked Marty if he could have a moment, and she was laughing when she told him to get back to her.

"Hello. I see that you feel better." He nodded at Chris and sat when she asked him to. "There has been a lot of speculation about you. Did you know that?"

"No. I don't know.... Did you do this?" She shook her head and then nodded. "As clear as ever, I see."

Her laughter filled the large room. Sterl liked these women, even respected them. Chris was a grand witch, the most powerful being on earth. And here she sat in torn jeans that he was sure were from working rather than fashion, with an odd little woman dressed entirely in Lego print, from the top of her head to the bottom of her feet, he was sure.

"What I mean is, I had some help with it. From some other beings that are happy that you helped them out." He asked her who that might be. "Richard for one. He's grateful to you for a lot of things, but mostly for not calling him on his bad behavior when he was here before. And the faerie queen. She would like for you to paint her sometime. She has it in her head that you'd do a good job of it."

"I'd like that. There really is a faerie queen?" Chris nodded. "Why? I mean, I've only just looked around a little, but this is a great deal."

"You deserve it. And I think there will be more coming your way. It's for what you're about to do as well." He asked her what that might be. "I cannot tell you as yet. You'll find out soon enough, but for now, it must remain a secret. Not harmful. I think you've had enough of that for several lifetimes. That brings me to the next point of why I'm here."

As she told him what she needed of him, he pulled a pad of paper and a pencil from the desk in front of him. He was sure that it hadn't been there before, the paper or the desk, but he took notes on what she was telling him. And each time she gave him information, he felt his need to paint double. Sterl was going to be very busy from now on, it appeared.

CHAPTER 11

"I don't understand." Marty looked over at the lawyer for the estate of Rose Baldwin, previous owner of the desk that she'd opened a few weeks ago. "This is her family's. They should...I don't know, but they should at least want the cash if nothing else."

"They cannot." The attorney, a stiff sort of man, sat there staring at them like he thought them beneath him. "If there is nothing else, I'll be on my way."

"There is plenty else, and you're going to sit right there until we get this figured out." She felt her face heat up when she spoke, and looked at Noelle when she laughed. "This desk was left at our shop, with money and other personal items in it that belong to this woman's family. What the hell are we supposed to do with it?"

"Frankly, I don't care. Mrs. Baldwin was a...I would call her stern. However, she wasn't the person that she's being made to look like. I can tell you that she tried, but things happened. And over the years they drifted apart. Mrs. Baldwin left instructions in her will that her children were not to get any form of a settlement from the estate, and once they went through the household and picked out one item each, the rest would be given away or destroyed. By the way, I have other pieces, a great many of them,

135

that should you want them, they can be yours as well. You'll just have to come to the house and pick them up before next Friday, when the house is being torn down."

"I still don't understand how the desk got to our shop." That's what Marty wanted to know as well, and was glad that Noelle asked. "I came into work one day and it was sitting on the loading dock. I'm assuming, from what you're telling me, that the family would have been the only ones to have been able to take this thing out of the house. Why pick that and not take it?"

"I couldn't tell you, and even if I had an idea why, I wouldn't tell you. They were to take one thing. This person took that, did so with the understanding that they'd get nothing else. What he did with it after that was entirely up to him. That is all they're to receive from the estate, and perhaps he decided that he didn't want it after all. Then with that, he took it to your shop to be resold." He stood up. "I really must be going. If you would be so kind as to have your attorney look this agreement over and send it to my office, then the matter will be closed. Good day to you, ladies."

Marty looked over at Noelle and laughed. This was insane. Not only were they a good deal richer for this thing, but they were going to be able to take whatever else from the estate they wanted as well. Noelle cleared her throat and stood up.

"Okay, we know who they are. The Baldwins, correct?" Marty nodded. "We'll take all the furniture, call them up, and see if they want it before we sell it. There has to be something there that they want."

"We can't do that." Noelle asked her why not. "It's in the contract here. Once we sign off on this, we can pick up the furniture but we cannot contact any member of the Baldwin family. She must have been one hell of a mother to do this to her own kids."

"Or the kids were little shits and deserved it." There was

136

that, Marty thought. "I don't know, Marty. I hate to think that these people won't have anything of their mother's. Not even a picture or anything."

"I don't like it either, but we did all we could. I mean, the money will be nice to buy up more things to sell. And the other things in the stupid desk will be a nice addition to the shop as well. I think that we should get what we can from the house and sell it. The money could go to something else, like supplies for the nursing home or shelter. We could even have a wing put on the library if there's enough of it. Anything is possible."

They planned what they were going to do, and they prearranged to go to the house with an officer so that there would be no trouble. Also, they'd called Tanner to come and read over the paperwork to get it approved. She was still sort of upset about the way things were working out for the family, but when Tanner arrived, he had Noah with him. He explained to them what he'd been able to find out while Tanner read things over.

"Not a nice family. There are four children, all adults now, and they have children of their own. Apparently when Mark Baldwin, their father, passed away, the children thought that they'd have their mother put in a nursing home and they'd take over the company and house. As you can tell, that didn't sit well with Rose. She was only in her late fifties at the time and of sound mind. Still was, as far as I thought, even well into her eighties." Marty asked why they'd do that. "Money hungry? Brats? Who knows the way of children nowadays? But she did turn the company into one of the richest in the world. Doubled the growth of it after the first five years, and went on to do more than most in her position would have done for the community as well. She was a good person."

"So, she had enough of them because of that. Seems sort of harsh, don't you think?" Noah said there was more. "They didn't give up, I'm taking it."

"No, they did not. The oldest, his name was Mark as well, decided that he'd try and buy up all the shares he could and force his mother out. He mortgaged his house a couple of times through different banks. Sold all his stocks in other companies to make it work, and even did some things that were far from legal to do it. The problem was, there were no stock holders to buy from. Rose owned it all." Marty laughed. "Yes, you think it's funny, but he did not. A few days after his house was taken, as well as his wife leaving him, he tried to kill his mother. He was arrested and died recently in prison. But that didn't stop the rest of them from continuing. Rose began to finally see her children for what they were. Horrible people that were only out for the money and nothing more. They broke ties when she told them that she'd taken them out of the will. She sent them copies so that they'd know she meant business. They were, in a word, fucked."

"I see. She tried to make amends too, didn't she?" Noah nodded. "What makes people think that what is yours should be theirs as well? I mean, she was smart as well as brave enough to run a company and make it work. Why did her children think that they needed it all?"

"According to Rose—and yes, I did know her for a time— no matter what she did, they'd want more. And when her grandchildren came along, she would have to pay to see them. Thousands of dollars too, just for a few minutes of their time. It got to the point where they were just as bad as their parents, and she washed her hands of them all." Noelle said that was sad. "It is. And what she's done, she did so because it was all they wanted from her, money. And in the end, they got nothing."

"I hope that she did something good with the money." Noah said that she had and smiled. "Good. I'm so glad. And now we're going to use the money we make off the sale of the furniture to make something good come out of it too. Like a wing on the library. Perhaps we'll call it, The Rose Baldwin Wing."

"She'd like that. She was an avid reader." Noah stood up and started for the door before turning back to her. "I would check each piece before you put it out on your floor. There might be other treasures there as well."

For some reason, Marty thought there was going to be a great deal more. And memories too, she thought. Some good ones that would have been from when Rose's husband was alive.

"This is all right." Tanner sat down with her and Noelle a few minutes later. "There is a clause in this that states should you find anything else in the furniture or anything else you were to take from the house, it is yours. I'm not sure how much more you'll find, but I'd be careful with whatever you remove from there."

"Noah said the same thing." He nodded but looked perplexed. "What is it? You seem worried. Should we not sign this?"

"No, you should. I was just wondering how Mrs. Baldwin knew you were going to take the furniture. I mean, her attorney brought this with him, right? You had no idea the offer was going to be on the table?" Marty and Noelle both said they'd had no idea. "Yes, but this paperwork, it's like the both of you and she discussed what was going to happen, and it's filled out like you had a prior agreement. I'm sure he was hoping you would, but you should notice the date at the top. Anyway, sign it and I'll take it to him on my way home. He's still at the hotel."

After Tanner left them, Noelle sat down. Their copy of the paperwork had been given to them, and Marty stared at hers without really seeing it. It wasn't until Noelle said her name that she realized she'd not even considered how late it was getting.

"It was dated a month ago." She asked Noelle what she meant. "The paperwork. It's dated a month ago. A few days before I got the desk at the back of the shop. She knew. Or someone did."

"Are you sure?" Noelle showed her the date. "This was before I even came to town. I mean, I wasn't even in the shop

139

until after you found it. Yet here is my name right alongside of yours. What's going on?"

"I don't know, but I'm not going to look into it. I think, and this is just me, we should just let it go. For now, anyway." Marty started to argue, but Noelle put up her hand. "You're new to this family, but I have to tell you, some strange shit is always going on, and I've learned just to let it go. Otherwise, you go nuts trying to figure it out. Like your house. That is some crazy shit there too."

Yes, it was, and Marty thought the other woman was right. Time to let it go and move on. Whatever they found? Well, she wasn't going to stress about that either.

~~~

Sterl finished the canvas and stood back to look at it. He'd never stretched his own canvas before and was quite proud of it. There were a few places he knew he could have done better, but all in all, he liked it. Setting it aside, he pulled the next frame to the table just as the door opened. He was glad to see Randal as he'd not seen him much lately.

"Classes were dismissed early because of weather." Sterl asked him if it was bad out. "Yes. I guess we're to get about six or seven inches of snow today. I went to the house and Alta said you were out here. This is amazing."

"Thanks. I love it. It's so nice to be able to just have space. What are you up to?" He told him nothing, but that didn't sound right. "Would you like to go into town with us later? We have to go to the bank for Marty to sign off on a few things there. Then we were going to have some dinner out. You should join us."

"I don't want to intrude." Sterl told him he wouldn't be intruding. "Okay, then. If you won't mind, I'd love it. I came by to talk to you about a couple of things you might know the answer to, at least I'm hoping so."

Sterl sat down too when Randal pulled out a chair. After

140

giving him a bottle of water, Sterl waited. One thing about Randal, he'd speak when he had something to say, and not before. Sterl was thinking about the canvas again when he finally spoke.

"There is this little girl in my class. Her name is Heather. Just about the cutest little thing you've ever seen, and polite, like Mom taught us to be." Sterl nodded. "Anyway, as you know, I have this area in my room for food and such. They can have what they want out of it, some even take some of the things home over the weekend to have so they won't starve, I think. Even a couple of them take things for younger siblings."

"I think that's about the best idea that I've heard for a teacher to do. You're a good man, Randal." He only nodded, staring at his water bottle. "I'd like to donate to it if you'll allow me to. Perhaps some gloves and hats too. Some of my students rarely had those to use."

"Doug donated a great deal of money to it. I have more should I need it. Lately, I've taken to packing up weekend bags for those that I think could use it. It's not much, but I think it keeps food in their bellies until they come back to class on Monday. I'm sort of concerned about the holidays. They'll be without those subsidies for a couple of weeks." Sterl said they'd think of something to help. "Thanks. Back to Heather. I think she's living alone."

"Alone? You mean, you think her parents have left her here?" Randal didn't say anything but got up to pace. "Randal, what makes you think she's alone?"

"When the New Year started, she was forever bruised. I mean, even her little face and arms. Then as the year went on, I noticed that she started to lose weight. A great deal of it for one so small. And there were the dark circles under her eyes." Randal got himself another bottle of water and sat down and looked at him. "Then over the last few weeks I've noticed that, while not heavier, she isn't hurt anymore. Her clothing is cleaner as well. I know you're going to say that she's finally getting help, but I don't think that's it. I think she's doing it for herself. There is also an improvement in her grades."

"So, you think they left her to do whatever people do when they leave children. What about her running away? Maybe she's living on the streets or something." Then he thought of what Randal had said. "No, that'd not be right either. She's cleaner, so that rules out living on the streets. Not to mention, someone might have seen her around."

"I need to do something." Sterl nodded. "Okay, here is what I needed to ask you about. What sort of trouble would I be in if I just showed up there? I mean, like a welfare check? I don't want to intrude, and I certainly don't what to get her into trouble."

"I'd say quite a bit if her parents are there, but none if you're sure that they're gone." Randal said he wasn't one hundred percent sold on his idea yet. "Yeah, me either. I think you're right, but not enough to get Heather in trouble. Also, if they are there, you might make them hurt her again."

"That's what I thought as well, but it's flipping cold out and I'm worried about her. I worry about all the kids, but this one, she has a part of my heart." Sterl asked him if there were any contact names on her paperwork. "I can't get any more than her address. And if I tell them why I want it, then that's not going to go over too well either."

"Did you talk to Joe or Trent?" He said that he didn't want to bother them with it. "But you want to bother me?"

"It's not that, but—" He told him he was only kidding. He was glad to help him. "Thanks. But I'm no closer than I was before."

They both looked at Marty when she entered the building. He loved the look on her face, as if she were caught with her hand in the cookie jar. When she asked them what she'd done, they both laughed. Randal told her what was going on.

"I can help you. If you want, that is." Randal thanked her

and asked what she could do. "Well, I'm new to the area. I was thinking of getting a babysitting job, and could go there with that query. You know, ask if they'd be interested in letting me sit for a few days for free. Then when I figure out if there aren't any parents or whatever, I can be gone and they'd be none the wiser. I saw it on a movie once."

"That might work." Randal got up to pace again. This time it was full of energy, like he was excited. "She lives in one of the worst parts of town. I mean, it's bad. But we'll be there should you have any trouble. Just.... I can't thank you enough for doing this for me."

As they got into the new SUV he'd picked up yesterday, Sterl watched Marty. She was excited to be doing this for his brother. And when they pulled up in front of the house, she didn't hesitate at all but went to the door like the plan had called for.

The little girl was so tiny next to Marty, and Sterl knew that Marty wasn't all that big. Tall, yes, but thin. When she went down on her knees to talk to her, Sterl wanted to go and help her out, but knew that he'd only frighten the child. Marty was apparently invited into the house and shut the door behind her.

"Do you think she's all right?" Sterl told Randal that he hoped so. "Me too. I never thought she'd just go in. I really don't know what I expected to happen, but it was not for her to be invited in."

A few minutes later, the little girl and Marty came out of the house. The child had a blanket wrapped around her and Marty was carrying a bag. Before they took a few steps, Marty bent and picked her up and brought her to the car. Once she was seated in the back seat with her and buckled in, Marty asked if they could go to Trent's house.

Do I want to know? She shook her head and told him to wait. *Are you all right? Do you...did you see them?*

Yes, they're there. Don't. Please. Not yet. He nodded and she looked at Heather. "We thought we'd have some lunch too, if you guys will buy."

Heather smiled but it was stiff. The blanket was tucked tighter around her by Marty, and Sterl looked at Randal. When he shrugged, Sterl started the SUV up and headed to the local diner for lunch.

I've contacted Trent. He told her good, still not sure what was going on. *They're dead. And I'd say they have been for a few days... maybe longer, I just don't know. Heather told me that she's not allowed to go into their bedroom... the only one in the house, by the way. I just looked in on them and the smell is bad. They have heat in there, but I don't think its anywhere else in the house.*

Food? When was the last time she ate? Marty told him she thought it had been a few days. *So Randal was right, there wasn't anyone there to help her out.*

No. I don't think, from looking around, that they were looking after her in the first place. Her little area was nice. There was clean clothing on the couch laid out, like she was ready to go to school, I'm betting. No food anywhere, but a few little snack bar wrappers. I don't know what killed them, but I can guess. The house smells of drugs and death.

They made sure lunch was a fun affair. Trent joined them with Joe a few minutes after they were served. The police arrived as well, but kept their distance. Sterl thought that Trent had asked them to do so. When Chloe showed up, dressed in her jeans and jacket, she sat with them.

"I love french fries, don't you?" She took one off Heather's plate when she offered. "Thank you so much. Now, I want to talk to you about a couple of things, Heather. And if you don't want to tell me, you can tell your teacher, Mr. Calhoun."

"My mommy and daddy won't wake up. I think they're dead." The last part had been whispered, but they all heard it well enough. "I didn't go in their room. I just let them rest in there. I get into trouble when I wake them up. But I don't think they're going to wake up this time."

"No. They aren't. Do you know what happened to them?" Heather told them about a good buy her daddy had made. "Do you remember when that was?"

"Yes. It was spelling test day. Tuesday." It was Saturday now, so that had been four days. "Not this one, but the one where we had to spell America."

"Christ." They all turned to Randal. "That was over a month ago…about five weeks now, I think. No, six. It's been six weeks since that test."

"I spelled it right too. Didn't I, Mr. Randal?" He told her that she'd done very well. "My daddy said that I wasn't to bother them. They were going to get it on. I don't know what that means, but they sure get noisy when it's going on. Then the next day, they never came out of their room. I never bothered them once. Not even when the man from upstairs asked me to go get them."

"What did he want?" Chloe asked again when she didn't answer. "It's all right. Just tell me what he wanted and I'll make sure that they don't bother you again."

"He wanted them to take a bath." Sterl felt his heart break for the child. To have lived for an entire month and a half with dead parents was more than even he could comprehend. "I didn't bother them."

She kept saying that. But before he could question it, Chloe did. "But you did go see to them, didn't you, love? You went in there and saw them."

Heather put her glass down and looked at her lap. He wanted to tell Chloe to back off, but she only shook her head at him and then spoke to them through their link.

There was a blanket pulled over them sometime after they were dead. Also, Mr. Zenick's wallet was pulled from the pocket of his pants, and there was a handwritten note from Heather as to what she'd taken. Not much, seemingly, but we found what was left of whatever cash she'd found in the house with a note of what she'd spent. And receipts.

145

A child saving receipts for dead parents so she could buy peanut butter and bread to eat.

"They never let me have things. I know that we can't have expensive things, but I needed to eat. I was so hungry that I could hear it in class, and the other kids made fun of me." Sterl looked at Randal. He looked as if someone had hit him right between the eyes. "I didn't buy the good stuff. Just the cheap peanut butter and the day-old bread. It was good, but got moldy really fast."

"I tell you what. You go on home with Mr. and Mrs. Calhoun. Trent and his lovely wife, Joe, will take care of you for a couple of days while we sort this out for you." Sterl looked over at Trent and he nodded. "Then when we're all finished, we'll see about getting you a warm place to stay. Do you have any grandparents? Maybe an aunt?"

"Aunt Laney, but I haven't seen her since I was little. She lives where people poop all the time, Daddy said." Sterl had no idea where that might have been until Heather laughed a little and corrected herself. "Not poop, craps. She plays craps for money."

"Vegas?" Heather nodded and smiled at him. "Your aunt is a craps dealer in Vegas? That's what you mean?"

"I think so. She does a card thing. Daddy didn't like her, but she's Mommy's sister. She would...sometimes she'd send me money for my birthday, but I never got to use it. It was for the household." Heather yawned and looked at Randal. "Mr. Randal, can I go home now? I'm tired, and I need to wash my underwear for school Monday."

"We'll get you set up, honey." Trent took her into his arms and stood there staring at them before he spoke. "Make this work out, will you?"

"Yes. I had no idea it was.... I knew there was something wrong, but I had no idea it was this bad." Trent put his hand on Randal's shoulder and told him he did the right thing. After they left, Randal looked at Sterl. "Thank you. From the bottom of my

146

heart, thank you."

"Anytime. Now we have to find a woman by the name of Laney in Vegas." He laughed. "Should be a piece of cake, I'm thinking."

CHAPTER 12

The bank manager was behind a little. Marty sat there wondering what it was going to be like to have money now that she was with Sterling. She wasn't a spend-for-no-reason kind of woman, but it would be nice to have boots and heavy coats when she wanted them. She looked around the big place. It was what banks thought they had to look like fifty years ago. Imposing. Rich. Safe. But whoever was in charge here had made some serious changes to the inside.

There were flowers on the desks. The tellers, she'd noticed, not only had one at their window, but a couple had them in their hair. They also greeted people by name and asked about their families.

One elderly woman that worked behind the desk looked like she might have been there when it first opened. She had suckers at her desk for anyone who wanted them. Dog treats for those who had pets in their cars waiting. Marty liked this place. It gave her a sense of welcome and safety.

"Sterling, Marty, thank you so much for coming in today. I have been so busy. Also, as per Mr. Sullivan, the money from the sales is in your joint account now. I also have a list of the people who purchased them, as well as their addresses, per Isaac's assistant. Terrible shame about his family. Just terrible." Marty

149

thanked him and they sat down at the desk. Another man joined them. "This is the company attorney. He's here in the event you have questions about what we're about to tell you. Let's go in order of my list, that way I won't forget any details. Here is the amount of the check that we deposited."

Sterling stared at it then looked at the banker, Mr. Music. "This can't be right. I mean, it's wonderful, but I don't think this is correct."

Marty took the copy of the check and burst out laughing. Gavin, he insisted that they call him, assured them that it was correct, minus the percentage that went to the estate.

"You don't understand. This is for four million seven hundred dollars." Gavin laughed and said he knew. "But there were only about a dozen paintings. I mean, I know that they all sold, but this is way more than I thought it would be."

"I'm to understand that you had a very good showing, and this proves that you're a wonderful artist. What I would recommend is that you get yourself a good investor. I'm sure that Tanner could get you squared away, but I'd find someone that deals well in the investments that you have as well." Sterling asked what investments. "I'm sorry. I'm getting ahead of myself. Let me do this in order, and I think you're going to understand better. That is the amount you were to receive from the work. Very good, sir."

The copy was put in her purse. Marty would look at it a lot later, she knew, but for now, she was going to pay attention to Gavin to see what else they needed to know. She was handed two cards to sign.

"These are for the accounts that you both will share. If you could sign them where it's indicated, I'll move on. This will allow you both access to the accounts, as well as put in a request for cards to go with it." Gavin looked at her. "You'll have Calhoun on yours, so let me know when that is final and I'll put that in as well."

"We're getting married the day after tomorrow." He congratulated them both and she smiled. "I'm sure that everyone in town is aware of it by now. Word travels fast in a town this small."

"It certainly does." Gavin took the cards back and put them in a pile to his left. Marty could see that his list was long, but the man was checking things off quickly. "Now, for the next matter. Isaac was in here a few days before he was murdered. He had me fix up a few things for him and to have some paperwork ready for you. I think he knew it was not going to end well, and he took steps to have his child taken care of, as well as his family business. He's left it to you."

"I'm sorry, what?" Gavin repeated what he'd said. "I can't take that. I mean, I was going to offer to buy it, but I can't just take it."

"Actually, he had made you a full partner in it. I do believe that's why the amount of the check is so large. You got his share in the sales as well. Then he changed a few things as well to make sure that you got the gallery if he should pass. You are the sole owner of Sullivan Gallery. I can add your lovely wife's name should you like, but he left it for you." Sterling looked pale. She wasn't sure how she felt about it either. "He was very sure of himself when he got here. Not that he was going to die, mind you, but of what he wanted. He also made sure that you had access to his accounts — well, both of you — and that you were to get all his personal belongs."

"His house, you mean." He nodded at her and said everything else as well. "I think you're trying to tell us something and you're hedging. I think you should skip right on down to it and explain."

"The little boy, his son, he made you the child's guardians." If he was still talking, Marty could no longer hear him. The little boy was theirs. She looked at Sterling when he snapped his

151

fingers in front of her face.

"Are you back?" She nodded, then shook her head. "Yeah, I feel the same way. Gavin went to get the paperwork that we're going to have to fill out to be his parents."

"We're raising Gavin too?" Her voice was loud, she knew, but no one said anything to her. "I'm freaking out a little here. I never dreamed in a million years that.... Why would he do that?"

"I don't know. But there is a letter to us both. I told Gavin that we'd read it when we got home. And since Benson is still with my mom and dad, we can take him home now. There are some things we'll have to sign, but he's our son as of the moment we leave here." She sat there while the banker explained things once he returned. She supposed she should have listened, but her mind wasn't working correctly.

They had millions of dollars now, a business, as well as a child. Marty put her hand on her belly and wondered about the one she carried. This was just too much for her to take in. She stood up, and both men did as well, then she asked where the bathroom was. Running in the direction she was told, she knew she was never going to make it.

She was sitting on the floor in the stall when she heard her name. Marty knew who it was; Christine had been coming to the shop every day just to hang out with them. She had grown to love the woman as much as she did anyone else in the family.

"Are you all right, my dear? TJ is about to come in here to slay dragons for you should you need him." Marty laughed. "There you go. Come on out here and have a word or two with me before Sterling breaks the door down."

"I was suddenly overwhelmed by everything." She came out of the stall and went to the sink to wash up. "I suppose you heard that we're going to raise Benson. That little boy. He's lost so much for someone so young."

"Yes, but he'll be loved by all of us. A readymade family that loves him will take care of some of the pain of it. And not that I don't think it's a great loss, because it is, but being so young, he'll not hurt as much as someone, say my age." Marty nodded and turned to look at her future mother-in-law. "You're still a little pale, child. Have a seat on the counter and let me get my heart rate under control."

She sat on the counter and put her hands on her lap. There was so much running around in her head that she had no idea where she should begin. Marty looked at Christine and smiled.

"Sterling made millions off his showing, and now owns the gallery. We're going to be parents to Benson, as well as our own child. The house changes to suit us, which means that it'll have the nursery as well as Benson's room all complete by the time we get home. It'll be perfect as well. I'm a partner in an antique shop with Noelle, and we've just taken the furniture of a very wealthy and sad woman, who may or may not have hidden more treasures in her things." Christine told her welcome to the family. "The wedding is soon and I have no one to invite to it, no family. Also, I've no money of my own, save for the few things that are in the furniture we find. If there is any. I'm not the type of woman that people like Sterling marries."

"I'm so glad that you're going to raise that little boy. He'll need you both. And someday, I'm hoping soon, you will have a child of your own. But with Sterling and you being different, perhaps that's just the point. You're perfect for him, I think. And you should know that anything that we have, you have. And that would include Sterling's money. I'm sure that he's told you that." She nodded. "Good. He's a good man that has had some very difficult times of it. That too, I'm sure he's shared with you. But what you don't know, or don't understand, is that you brought him back to us. Sterling used to be such a wonderfully happy young man. Vibrant, full of life. He taught children and loved every moment of it. Every aspect of being their teacher. Then a monster came along and took that from him. Hurt him so badly that even as his mom, I'll never understand. Nor do I think I want to. But you've given him back to us. You've given him that spark that we all missed. You say you have nothing. Well, from where I stand, I think you've given us more than anyone could have by loving us, and especially my Sterling. By the way, I love that you call him that."

"I've never loved before. Never had anyone care for me like he does. For that matter, you all have. I'm so glad that he found me." Christine hugged her. It was heartfelt, Marty could feel it, and she hugged her back. "I'm ready to go back out now."

"Of course you are. But you should know that the rest of the family has shown up. They can feel—well, Trent can mostly—but we all knew you were upset, so just let them hug you and ask after you. They'll feel better for it." As they were going to the door, Christine paused again. "Oh, and you should expect something different from James. He's...well, he's James. As much as I love that old man, he can be the most irritating of all the men I know."

She had no idea what to expect when she came out the door. It was on the tip of her tongue to ask Christine if they could wait them out. But suddenly she was being hugged tightly and hands were patting her on the back. Love. This was just what love felt like when it was freely given. Then she looked at her grandda-in-law.

"I have a favor to ask of you. Well, all of you." James wiped his nose with his hanky then nodded at her. "I'd like to call you what Sterling does. Grandpa for you, if you'd allow it. And the others, Grandma, Mom, and Dad. I already think of the others as brothers and sisters."

"It'll come with a price. This thing you want to do." She nodded, expecting no less from this older man. "I'll expect to be invited to dinner weekly, and I want to be asked to babysit, even if you have nowhere to go but to the mailbox. I've never had a great grandchild before, so I'm hoping that you'll make me toe the line when I mess up with them."

"Will you love them?" He said of course he would. "Then you can't ever mess up as far as I'm concerned. And I've never been a mother before either, so we can learn together."

"Good deal." He hugged her then, picking her up in his arms and then swinging her around the room. When he set her on her feet, he kissed her cheek. "I'm gonna have some fun now, I think. Yes, sir, I will."

~~~

Sterling was sitting in the chair by the desk. He'd been up for hours, just sitting there waiting for the sun to come up, his mind too busy to settle on one thing, so he let it roam. Looking around when the door behind him opened, he looked at Noah and Benny.

"How are you?" He nodded at Benny and smiled at the man. "You look like a man who has a great deal on his mind. We thought we'd come by and add more to it."

"Maybe it'll make a nice distraction. I've heard from the faerie queen and a few other royals over the last few days. Did you know that there is a lineage for each and every part of the earth?" Benny told him that he was learning that as well. "I've been commissioned to paint them, and for a great deal of money. I was letting things work around in my head about that as well."

Noah sat down while Benny roamed the snowy deck. He was a good man with a lot on his mind as well, Sterl would think. When he finally settled in the chair by the fire ring, Sterl looked at Noah.

"The little girl that your brother is keeping an eye on, did you know that she's part faerie?" Sterl told him that nothing would surprise him anymore. "Yes, I would imagine that you've had a lot more than most men thrown at you. I came to tell you that I've

155

found her aunt. She is not at all like her sister."

"I didn't figure she would be. I've been thinking about her as well. And I've concluded that she's a mate to one of my other brothers." Noah nodded. "I thought so. And I have a feeling that it's going to be Randal. He already has a connection to the child. That way they'll come together for her."

"Not as easily as you might think. Laney Price is.... You know my Joe and how stubborn she can be? Well, Laney is much more. I'd say she might even be more stubborn than I am." Sterl asked if she was on her way. "Not that I'm aware of. I think you'll find out that she has a great deal of mistrust when it comes to her sister and her husband. I don't believe that she thinks they're really gone. They might have done this to her before."

"They were sick bastards." Noah agreed. "So, how do we get her here? I'm assuming that you might have a plan in all this."

"I do. But you aren't going to like it." Sterl leaned back in the chair and regarded his friend. "First of all, she doesn't have the means to come here. Not that she's broke, but she won't touch her savings account for any reason. She came from a very poor family, and decided that she won't do without."

"I can understand that, but this is her niece." Noah shook his head. "You said that the woman in the house was her sister. Why won't this be her niece?"

"Heather is her half-sister. Laney only just found out about it a few months ago. Laney's father is the child's father, and her stepmother is the mom. Very complicated, I think. The reason that the Zenicks had her is anyone's guess. But I'm going to figure that as well. You might say that this is a mission for me. I'm bored." Sterl laughed and Noah cocked a brow at him. "You think my boredom is funny?"

"No. But I remember something that my mom used to say to us as kids. A bored wolf is a wolf that is going to be in trouble. I would imagine that as a bored vampire, you can get into all sorts of trouble. Are you, Noah? Going to get into trouble?" He grinned at him. "Ah, so you've considered that, have you?"

"A little. Which brings me to why I'm here. I don't think you should take the little girl out to her sister. You and Marty should go alone." He asked why Randal wasn't going. "He needs to figure that part out on his own. And he will, but that will need to be his doing. Leave Heather here when you go see her sister, then tell Laney what you've been able to find out. I know that isn't much, but you'll have more when you leave."

"You know more than the police?" Noah nodded and looked over at Benny. "He found it for you."

"Yes, Benny is very good at digging, I've discovered. And he's finding things for me all the time now. We make a good partnership. But this woman, she'll come back with you to sign paperwork. That's the only reason that I've figured will bring her back. As I said, she is most untrusting." Sterl said he could do that. "Also, and this is the part where I think you're going to be upset with me, I've set you up for a gallery opening. It's in mid-July, so you should be able to paint more before then, correct?"

"I don't know." Noah said nothing. "The work I do, I thought for some reason that it would go away, the darkness of my work, but I have so many things rushing around in my head that I'm sort of afraid of it."

"That, too, is understandable. You've been afraid for a long time. And the things that are rushing around in there, they'll make great paintings that while few will understand, everyone will love." Sterl wasn't so sure about that either. "Sterling, whether you paint or not, I think you're happy now."

"Yes, very much so, and I'm in love." Noah smiled at him. "We're going to raise Benson as our own. We won't change his last name...Marty and I decided that someday he might like to take over the gallery again, so a Sullivan is running it. But that'll be up to him as well. We read the letter last night and have decided to save it for Benson. Isaac wrote about his love for the little boy and how he'd come to the decision to leave him with us. I think he might need that, just to feel better about what his dad did for him."

"Good. I think that's a very good move. I knew you were smart." Sterl just laughed. "The little girl. You'll help her? You'll go and find her sister for her? She might not be easy."

"None of my life is easy. Falling in love, that was easy, but the rest of my life? No, not easy at all. But, in answer to your question, yes, I'll do this. There really is a person I'm to talk to out there about a show?"

"Oh yes. That was set up long before Benny found out about the child and her sister." Noah stood up. "Go. Paint. Then when you are finished, I'd like to see the faerie queen's painting. She is someone that I admire as much as I do you."

Long after Noah and Benny left and Sterl had gone into the house, he sat in his chair. He wanted to go out and paint…it was something that he had planned when getting up early. But the snow falling in soft flakes and the sun just turning it a nice soft shade of pink had him still sitting. There was so much going on in his head that he reached for the pad and pen that he'd found in the bottom of one of the drawers a few days ago.

He didn't think about what he was doing…just putting the pen to the paper made him relax a little. By the time he was turning to another page to fill, he was feeling like he was onto something. Sterl never looked at the drawings, or whatever it was he was putting there, but closed his eyes and let his mind take his hand to wherever he wanted it to go. By the time he could no longer hold the pen in his hand—it was cramping severely—he was also exhausted.

Leaving the pen and pad on his lap, Sterl leaned back in his seat and closed his eyes. Sleep took him gently. He knew on some level that he might slip out of the chair, but for now, he was tired and relaxed. Nothing was going to harm him here.

When he woke he was covered up by the coverlet that had been on the couch. Stretching, he looked at the grandfather clock that he'd found on one of his trips with Noelle. It was nearly three o'clock, which meant that he'd been asleep for nearly nine hours. Getting up, he saw the envelope on his pad, as well as the pen. Picking up the note, he read it aloud.

"I don't know if you are aware of it, but there is a nice comfy bed upstairs. I'm glad you got some much needed rest, however. Anyway, I'm at the shop with Noelle, and a package arrived for you this morning. Don't know who it's from, but Alta said you'd like it. Love, M."

Going to the kitchen, Sterl stretched again. His wolf curled along his body, sort of telling him that he was rested as well. Upon entering the big room, he saw the package and the large platter of food that Alta had in her hand. Food first, then package, his growling belly told him.

"It's from the queen. The witch one, not the faerie. Though she will be more than likely sending you one as well. Miss Chris said that you'd need this and I was to give it to you first thing." He thanked her. "Myra said to tell you that you should paint the second one. Don't know what that means, but I was to pass it on to you."

"I was sketching. I don't normally do that, but I had to today." He ate the entire platter of ham, sausage, biscuits, and gravy. Drinking down two glasses of orange juice, he pulled the package toward him and took the knife that Alta handed him. "Am I going to know what this is, you think?"

"I don't know. It's warded so that I can't tell. But you go on ahead and open it. I asked if you needed to do it somewhere safe, but she said anywhere would be fine." He didn't want to think about why she'd need to ask if it would be safe, but cut the tape holding the lid together. "Careful now. You don't want to cut yourself."

Laying the knife aside, he carefully opened the tissue paper inside. When he looked into the box, he wasn't at all sure what he was looking at. When he looked at Alta, thinking she'd have an idea, he was shocked to see her expression.

"Alta? What is it?"

She said "Oh my," and he stood up. But before he could move to her, the blast of heat took his breath away, then darkness engulfed him.

CHAPTER 13

Marty had just set down a pretty vase that they'd gotten from the house. She stepped back and then doubled over in...not pain, it wasn't painful, but it did take her breath away. And then heat filled her, from the tip of her toes to her hair. She even reached up to touch it, just to make sure that she wasn't in flames. Marty sat down just as Noelle came toward her.

"You all right?" Marty told her that she thought so. "You sort of blinked out there for a moment. I mean, not disappeared, but you were just red hot. Are you sure you're all right?"

"Yes, I think so, and I was hot, but.... It wasn't like I was on fire, but it was hot. I don't know what happened." She suggested that she talk to Sterl to make sure that he was all right. She tried. "It's like I'm touching a wall. Is that bad?"

"Can you feel him?" She said that she could, but there was a wall. "Not that I'm trying to freak you out, but that's telling you that he's not dead, just unconscious. Keep trying and I'll close up and take you home. You might find that he's resting still."

He'd been asleep when she'd gotten home last night, and then again this morning. She was sure that he was exhausted after everything that had been going on, but she missed sleeping with him. He was her rock and someone that she needed badly, no matter if it was to simply cuddle up next to him.

She hated that Noelle was going to close the shop to take her home, but she didn't have a car and Marty was sort of nervous about what she'd find when she got there. By the time she got in touch with Sterling, she was nearly frantic with all the crap that she had in her head.

I got a package from Chris Bentley. I think she tried to cook me. She told him that she'd felt it as well. *Are you all right? I'll murder her if you're hurt.*

No, I'm fine.

Great. What was in it? You don't think she'd try to harm us, do you? He told her that he didn't think so. *I'm almost home. Noelle is bringing me.*

A car. Damn it, I forgot. I got you one yesterday, and they're undercoating it for you. Ohio weather is rough on the underbelly of cars, but you probably already knew that. She asked him what he'd gotten for her. *An SUV like mine. Loaded. I can't have my future wife running around with a cheap vehicle. Besides, they cut me a deal for getting two of them. I'm sorry. I should have told you.*

It's all right. I've never had a new car before. In fact, I don't think I've had a new anything. This is so wonderful of you. He told her that he loved her. *And I love you. We're pulling in the drive now.*

Telling Noelle that she'd talked to him, Marty could tell that she was just as relieved as she was. Getting out, she wasn't at all surprised to see Trent and his dad stepping out of their own cars. They told her that they'd felt Sterling pass out as well.

They were greeted in the house by Sterling and Alta, who had a pad of paper and a pen. After hugging Sterling and seeing to the rest of them, she asked Alta what she needed.

"The household would like to decorate something for themselves for the holidays." The household? Honestly, she thought that Alta was the only staff they had and said as much. "No, you have a great many faeries and brownies working here. A few younger witches. They love what you've done to the house, but they'd like to know if they can decorate a tree for themselves, or will you be doing that?"

"I don't know. I mean, I've never had the means to decorate before, but that part is all done. I do think a house this large could take a lot more decorations, don't you think?" Alta nodded and smiled. "I don't have a problem with them doing it. Did you ask Sterling?"

"He said that he wanted to go all out, but that I should ask you. Mr. Sterling said that whatever you decided, it was going to be good. He did request that their tree be put up in the living room. I asked and he said that if we want to put a small one in every room, it was fine by him."

"Well, then I think you should all go for it. I'd like to go all out as well. You start whenever you wish. I guess we're going to his parents' for Thanksgiving dinner." She said they were going to start when they left for the dinner. "All right. Oh...I don't know how to cook. I mean, I've worked in a restaurant for years, but I never got the hang of cooking. I'm supposed to bring something to dinner. I told them I had no idea, but Christine said that I could whip something up with you."

"I'd be honored to help you, miss." Marty started away then turned back when Alta said her name. "The little boy's room is finished as well. He's coming today, I've heard."

"Yes. They had to make sure that the paperwork was all correct before we could take him. And he's had his physical too. I think they're afraid Sterling and I will break him or something." Alta was still laughing when she went to the kitchen. The pad of paper that she had was gone, and Marty thought that odd, but then so was the house, to say the least.

Trent was seated at the desk with his brother behind him. TJ was sitting on the couch talking about some piece of property that he'd found that he wanted to buy. She sat next to him as he explained what they were doing.

163

"There's the little place, used to be a cobbler, I think. Anyway, I was thinking that I need it." She asked him what he needed it for. "I don't know. I just need it. Like women and shoes."

"I don't collect shoes, bags, or dresses. I had three pairs of pants, four shirts, and a pair of shoes when I came here. Of course, now I have more, but I didn't buy them." He laughed. "Now what is so funny?"

"You're adorable. But I was thinking that I could purchase the building because it's for sale. I know that sounds silly, but there is a bigger grocery store coming to town, and that building is on the other side of the store. Which, by the way, I own as well." She said that she'd heard that. "I can't make it work. It's open and all, but I'm just not the grocery store type. I talk too much."

"Really? You? Talking too much? Nah. You never shut up, but you don't talk too much." He frowned and asked her the difference. "None. I was pulling your leg. But you usually get around to whatever it is you're heading toward. I enjoy being with you because of that."

"I'm not sure you gave me a compliment." She kissed him on the cheek. "All right then, that will make up for it. By the by, did you feel whatever hit our Sterl?"

"I did. We've not discussed what it might have been yet. He did tell me it was from the witch, but nothing more." He told her it was magic. "Magic? I don't think we need any more, do you?"

"Don't know. I would like to say that you don't, but you never know. That Chris, the witch, she can see things we can't. Not that she can tell us about them, but she knows them. Perhaps this was her way of keeping you safe for whatever is coming." She told TJ that she thought they'd had enough. "Me too, but the more you think like that, the more things just come out of nowhere. Be prepared, is what I say. You might go a long time ready and nothing happens, but you put down your guard and bam, it hits you right between the eyes."

Good advice.

The building that TJ had come here to look at was purchased. She thought a buck was a good price, but TJ had wanted them to give it to him. Both Trent and Sterling had told him he got a good deal. The man had all the money in the world and bitched about a buck. He winked at her as he was complaining again about the high prices.

They ended up staying for dinner, as did the rest of the family. It was a few days until Thanksgiving, and they were to marry in the morning. Things were going fast, she thought, but loved every moment of it. It wasn't until later that they talked about the gift from Chris.

~~~

The box had a single flower in it. It was a beautiful rose and looked like it had only just been picked. When Sterl took it out of the box, he laid it on the table and went to find a vase to put it in. He was sure there was one here, but finding it might be a problem.

"Did you see this?" He turned to see an envelope that Marty was holding. "It's addressed to us both. I wonder what it is."

He had her open it while he searched in vain for the vase. Finally, after ten minutes of looking, he put it in a glass with water and went back to the table. Picking Marty up, he sat her on his lap and took the note when she handed it to him.

"It says that we're going to need the magic enclosed. What do you suppose that means?" He said he had no idea, but it had knocked him on his ass when he got it. "Yeah, me too. It was.... Well strange is a tame word to use around this family. But it also says that I'm wolf and I'm not. Joe told me how that would work, and I think I'd remember you doing those things to me."

"So would I. I'm not sure, but we can figure that one out. Want to go out back and test it?" The snow had been falling for several hours now, and was piled up good around the house. But he also knew that tomorrow and the next day it was going to be in the mid-fifties, and most of that would melt away. Ohio weather wasn't the finest if you wanted consistency. "I promise you, if it doesn't work, I'll come back in here and warm you up."

"I just bet you would." She stood up and went to get her coat, and he told her she'd not need it if she was a wolf. "But what if I'm not? I mean, it's what, like twenty-five out there?"

"There is another way that I can tell. Not nearly as much fun, but if you just let me sniff you, I can tell without you going outside." She asked him why he'd not said that in the first place. "I don't know. I just wanted to see you naked."

"Naked? In the snow?" He nodded and she laughed. "You're very strange. You know that? Strange indeed. All right, sniff me, and if I'm a wolf, we'll go out. Otherwise, we're staying in here where it's warm."

When he sniffed at her skin he knew. Licking her, tasting the wolf there on her, was like sipping a fine wine, smelling roses in their first bloom, and feeling a good paintbrush in his hand all at once. Lifting her chin up so that she could look at him, he smiled.

"I'm a wolf." He nodded. Her voice was low, almost a whisper. "What do I do now? I mean, how do I change?"

"Think of her. Just close your eyes and think about the wolf. Can you see her?" She nodded. "Good, now ask her to take you."

He fell back when she changed. The wolf only stared at him for several seconds before she sat down and cocked her head at him. Carefully, so as not to startle her, he touched his fingers to the top of her head, then ruffled her fur between his fingers.

"You're beautiful. Silver, you're a silver wolf. I've never seen one before." He touched his head to hers, feeling how thick her coat was. "You're beautiful. If you'll stand still for just a moment, I'll take your picture."

He got up and he thought of something. Turning, he looked

at Marty when she simply laid down. He reached out to her, letting her see that she could talk to him the way that he had before, and she laughed.

I had no idea how that worked. Thank you. I've seen your wolf, I thought you were all gray. He told her that it depended on the region they were from and how many other wolf packs they'd blended with. *Oh, that makes sense. Are we going outside?*

"Yes but let me take a few shots of you so that I can show you when we come back in." She posed for him. It was comical, really, seeing her try to walk on four feet rather than two. Then when she was ready, more than ready, he opened the door for her and she took off like a shot. Before he could shift and go with her, the faerie queen stepped out of the shadows.

"She'll be hidden when necessary in this weather, and not easy to detect in the warmer weather as well. She will be good at hiding." He asked if someone was coming that she needed to be hiding from. "Yes."

When nothing else was forthcoming, he decided to let it go. Sterl knew that he should ask, but right now he just wanted to play with his mate. He did ask if it was urgent that she hide now, and she told him there was enough time. Nodding once, he let his own wolf take him.

The ground was thick with the snow. There was more than six inches of it, and he could see just where Marty had gone. He laughed when he realized that she was leaping around, and made his way to her by following the obvious foot path she was taking. When Sterl found her, she was watching the deer that came to graze on their property in the summer.

We let them roam here where it's safe for them. In the warmer months, we put out salt and other things for them to eat so that they'll stay. And Randal grows oat for them too. She asked why they weren't running. *They know us. I mean, they know who I am. They'll need to get used to your scent. But they're waiting, I guess, for you to make a move.*

They're beautiful, aren't they? He said they were. *I saw other animals here as well. A bear too.*

He's a bear, not a shifter. So are the deer. There are some wolves about, most of them are in Trent's pack, but there are some wild ones as well, so learn to tell the difference. She laid down and he moved up to stand over her. *There are all kinds of shifters on the property all the time. Some are here to protect, others just need a place to run. They might live in the city or close to it and don't have what we have.*

They didn't move, either of them. A hawk came to see them, another shifter who was someone he'd known for a long time. A cat, a tiger specifically, visited them, but said very little other than to congratulate him on his mate and new baby. As the forest around them cleared out, people going to their homes, no doubt, he and Marty were alone for the most part.

Benson comes today. He told her that he thought he was on his way. *I know nothing about children. I mean, he's adorable and all, but I don't know how to take care of him.*

He's almost a year old so he won't be too bad, I don't think. And Grandma and Grandda said they'd come by and make sure that we don't hurt him. I don't think we will, but you know Grandda. Marty laughed with him. *As much as I'd like to make love to you right now, I think we should be headed back. Like you said, Benson will be here soon, and I'd like to not be frozen when I hold him.*

They made their way back to the house and stood on the porch for a few minutes after they were both themselves again. He held her to him, smelling the fresh scent of her wolf and the child that she carried. When Alta came out to tell them someone was coming up the drive, they went inside. He was going to be a father in a few minutes, and he was as excited as he'd ever been before.

His family arrived first. His parents and grandparents had gifts for Benson and for Heather, who was staying with Trent and

Joe for now. Then his brothers came in, each of them excited and ready to start being an uncle. The women had gifts too, some for Benson, but they didn't forget the newest member of the family. Heather got a doll and a case with clothing for it. Once they were all settled around the fireplace, he told them about Vegas and going out to do a show.

"You're really doing this. I'm so proud of you." Grandma hugged him several times while she stood with him. "I knew you could do this. Didn't I tell you?"

"You did. And once this show is set up, I was thinking that we'd make it a little honeymoon for the three of us while we're out there. Get used to being a family that travels." His mom volunteered to watch over Benson for them, so they could have more fun, and he told her that he'd think about it. "Also, there are some paintings that I've been asked to do. I'm going to be busy over the next few months. I never dreamed that I'd be saying this, but I'm loving being a painter. Thank you all for your support in this."

"We're just glad that you're back with us. We were worried there for a while." He told Elijah he'd been worried as well. "I'm glad that you're getting better too. I love having the old Sterl back with us."

The rest of them agreed, and he felt good. He had the best family in the world, and now he had a mate too. Sterl wasn't sure that life could get any better than this. Then the doorbell rang and he felt his heart skip a couple of beats. His son, their son, was here.

Benson had been crying. His face was tear stained, his eyes puffy with it. When he asked the woman and man with him about it, Sterling was told he was upset, but they didn't know why. Sterl had a feeling he was missing the two people that he'd spent his life with up until now. He pulled him out of his coat and held him close.

169

"Hey, fella. You having a rough day?" Benson stared at him but didn't cry again. "My name is Sterling. You are going to live with us."

Benson looked around and smiled at Marty. It was a toothy smile, all three of his teeth showing. When he reached for her, Marty took him like a pro and Benson laid his head on her shoulder. Everyone stayed back, he noticed, and was glad for this bonding time alone.

"We've brought you some things to start out with. There are some records from his physician that says he has a reaction to a certain brand of diapers." Sterl nodded and made note of the brand. "Also, for the next several months, we'll be coming by unannounced to make sure that he's doing well and that you're not having any troubles. I don't think you will, not with a supportive family like this one, but we still have to do it."

"I understand. And we have a few questions of our own, if you don't mind." They weren't all that difficult, but Tanner had told him it would go a long way in building trust with the system. "Do we need to take him to the same doctor? Is he on any medications that we should know about? And we plan to go to his home and wonder if we should bring back pictures of his parents for his room, or wait?"

"All very good questions. No, he can see your own doctor, but I'd tell them about his pediatrician. No medications, though I'm to understand that he's teething still and might need a little gel on his gums at times. As for the pictures, I don't know the answer to that one. I'd speak to his doctor and find out what he wants to do. To me, I would think it would be fine, since you don't plan to keep from him that he's adopted, but you should ask." Sterl nodded. "Also, congratulations on your showing. I understand that it was a great success."

"It was, and thank you."

After she left, he sat down with Marty, who was still holding

Benson. His family looked ready to pounce, and he asked if anyone wanted to hold him. Sterl laughed for ten full minutes when every one of them stood up and raised their hands. Even little Heather wanted her chance.

Benson was passed around then. His mom told him stories about him, of course. Dad made promises of taking him to work with him. Showing him the ropes, he thought he said. Grandma asked him to please call her Grandma. Grandda held him without saying a word. Sterl asked him what was wrong.

"Nothing. I mean, not really. I have this beautiful little boy looking at me like you all did when you were about this age. Brings a man to tears to have someone look at him with so much trust and love in their eyes, don't you think?" Sterl nodded. "Him and me, we're going to get into so much trouble. I'll have him all primed up for the others when they come along. I just love this, more than I thought I would."

In a few months to a year, there would be four more great-grandchildren in the family. The twins that Noelle was carrying. His own child, as well as Heather. No one but Marty and he knew about the little girl, but they were going to be just as happy about her as they were the others. His family was the best there was.

When dinner was called, they sat around the table, all of them laughing and talking at once. Sterl held onto Marty's hand under the table, and was glad to have them all here. Benson was only the beginning, he knew, of a long and very happy year. Sterl could not wait for Christmas.

CHAPTER 14

Laney turned over her cards when everyone had placed their bets. She hadn't won this round, but that was fine by her. Sometimes, she knew, the house had to lose or people wouldn't come around. Two people got up from her table and two more sat. It had been like that all day, and she wondered what was going on that would have it so busy here on a Tuesday afternoon.

"Hello." She nodded at the man and woman and asked them to place their bets. "Oh sure. You'll have to help me a little, I've never done this before."

That line had been used a great many times over the years she'd been working here. But for some reason, she had a feeling that he wasn't trying to pull a fast one. After a quick lesson in how things worked, he bought fifty dollars in chips from her and laid them out in front of him. The woman did the same.

The woman won three hands and tripled her money. The man only won one, but she had to smile at how excited he got. He was still in the hole but he was having the time of his life, she'd bet. The table cleared but for the two of them.

"I'm Sterling Calhoun and this is my wife, Marty." The name sounded familiar, but she didn't remember as she dealt out another hand. "We're from Ohio."

Her hand froze in mid deal. Looking at him, she tried to think what the fuck he'd be doing here and what her sister had done now. Instead of asking him, which she wanted to do in the worst kind of way, she finished dealing out the cards.

"We have Heather, your sister." Laney put the cards down and stepped back from the table. It was a cue that would have someone come and take her table for her, that she needed a break. But as busy as it was, she was still standing there when the woman continued. "My name is Marty Calhoun, as he said, but I wanted to tell you that Heather is safe. And your other sister and her husband are both dead."

"How?" She told her about the drugs found in the house. "They're really gone? Both of them? And if you're lying to me, I'm not going to be happy."

The woman pulled out her phone and laid it in front of her. Laney moved closer so that she could see them. Her sister and her piece of shit husband. They were in caskets with flowers across them. When she moved her finger over the pictures again, there was a picture of Heather. She was as beautiful as she remembered her to be.

"My brother, he's her teacher, knew there was something wrong when Heather started coming to school with her clothing cleaned and her hair brushed. She was hungry all the time, but he has this set up in his room that provides for children that are less fortunate. Basically, we went to her home, hoping to find out what was going on, and thought they were gone. But Heather told my wife that she wasn't able to go into their bedroom, and Marty checked. The police were brought in a few minutes later." Laney asked if Heather had been hurt by them. "Previously, the doctor said that she had been, but she had no drugs in her system when she was taken to the hospital. My parents have petitioned the county to have her stay with them. She's well provided for, and adjusting easily."

"I can't.... She knows me, of course, but I haven't had a great deal of contact with any of them for years. As you've mentioned, she's not my niece but my half-sister. Sally Anne was also my half-sister." Sterling said they were aware of that. "I don't know what to do."

"We're here to help you."

She didn't say anything, but was relieved to have someone come and replace her. She must have looked worse than she felt, because her pit boss asked her four times if she was all right. She wasn't, but told him she was fine.

"Laney, is there somewhere we can talk?"

"No. I don't.... No, not yet. I need time to...." She started to walk away. "I'll contact you in a few hours. I get off at four."

The man handed her a card and she nodded without looking at it. She was in the break room when it hit her what had just happened. Sally Anne and Clay were dead. Heather was staying with people that she didn't know, and Laney wasn't even sure how to contact her stepmother to let her know, if she'd even care.

The rest of the afternoon was a blur. If someone had asked her what she'd done today, all she would have been able to do was stare blankly at them. She was glad now that she was off for the next two days, and decided that she wasn't going to answer her phone if it was from work. Hell, she might not answer it from anyone. Laney went home to her little apartment and sat in the corner with her blanket wrapped around her.

There had been a lot of calls to her phone over the last few days. None of them were numbers she knew. Nor did she listen to the voice mails. Sally Anne had done this before...pretended all sorts of scams to get her to come home, or at the very least, to send money. She'd done that for a while, helping out with rent and food, but even that got old when she figured out they were using it for drugs rather than anything that she sent it for. Then she found out about Heather.

Laney knew that her sister was a drug addict. She also knew

that Clay had been into more trouble than most hoods she met working in Vegas. But they were together, and that was all that mattered to them. Then one day, her stepmother had informed her that Sally Anne had a child.

"What do you mean, she has a child? She can barely take care of herself, much less an infant." Rosemarie told her that she thought that Sally Anne would make a great mother. "Of course, you would. You think that I'm a loser too. So, your opinion means shit to me. When did she have it?"

"You're always so quick to put her down. Why can't you be a little more like her and forgive occasionally?" The same thing she said to her all the time. She needed to be more like Sally Anne and Clay.

"Because I'm not a drug addict married to an equally stupid dope head. I also enjoy life too much to take drugs. Not to mention, having a roof over my head is sort of nice." Rosemarie told her that she loathed her. "Well, that's wonderful. I guess that your nomination for mother of the year award paperwork can hit the trash can."

"You're so mean. The least you can do since you won't share your money with us is provide a nice gift to the baby. Money is what they need." She had sent money after that, but only the one time. Two days after they had cashed the check, they were both arrested for being publicly intoxicated.

She stopped sending cards with money in it for the little girl too. They took the money and used it for things that didn't benefit the child. Laney wished that she'd had some way, any way, to have taken little Heather from them years ago.

Her cell ringing stirred her. Laney hadn't realized that she'd fallen asleep sitting there, and couldn't move well enough to go and get it. She hurt, her legs were tight, and her arms, from holding herself securely, were sore as well. By the time she got to her phone, it had long since stopped ringing and alerted her that she had a voicemail. Laney went to take a shower instead of bothering with it.

Three hours later, after taking a bath instead of a shower, Laney felt almost human again. There were several more missed calls, three from work, the rest from a number she didn't know, and more voicemails. She sat on her couch to listen to them. But instead, she looked at the card that she'd gotten from Sterling Calhoun. It was the same number that had shown up that she didn't know. Laney wasn't even going to speculate how he'd gotten her number.

She didn't want to call him, but knew that she had to. Her little sister was out there and might need her. Laney had decided not to call Rosemarie. It was just too much drama to deal with her, and besides, she was in no better position to raise Heather than Sally Anne was.

Laney was still trying to figure out how Sally Anne had ended up with Rosemarie's child. Their biological father was a horror of a man too, beating whoever got in his way, or even if someone was breathing the same air he was. The man hated people. There had to be a good reason for Rosemarie to have given up the child, and she was going to find out. Calling the Calhouns, she wondered if they had the information that she'd not been able to find.

~~~

Sterl hung up the phone and looked over at Marty, who was napping. She'd been doing that a lot over the last few days, and he was worried about her. He needed to wake her to let her know what he'd set up with Laney. But a few more minutes wasn't going to hurt, he thought, when he decided to think about what Laney had said.

He knew that she was aware of the child being her half-sister. But how it had happened, she had no idea. He did. Joe had found out for him when she'd started searching for it. It had only taken her a few hours to find out that as the mother and Sally Anne lived in different states, it was easy for them to both claim her on their taxes and with the welfare offices. Rosemarie had even gone as far as applying for a second Social Security card after Sally Anne had. It was a scam that was going to get the mother in deep trouble when it came out. And it would.

"Did you talk to her?" He nodded and laid down next to Marty when she spoke. "You're worried about me. Don't. I'm tired a lot, but I think it's more to do with the fact that I've never felt so safe before. I'm catching up."

"You promise that you aren't sick?" She told him that she felt wonderful, but tired, that was all. "Well, we're going to meet Laney for dinner in a couple of hours. She has a lot of questions. Do you suppose we should have brought Heather with us? I know that Noah said not to, but she might have been a little more receptive if we had."

"No. I think this way is better. And even he admitted that it was for the best. Joe was right in thinking that bringing her here and Laney rejecting her might have been too much on the little girl. Besides, your parents are having the time of their life with the kids." He knew that as well. "Oh, we're supposed to go and purchase some of those big candy bars for your parents. I think they want to give them to the kids for Christmas."

"I have a list that they want. Do you want to go with me to dinner? You can rest more if you'd like. I can wake you when I get back." He wiggled his brows at her, which made her laugh. "There's my baby. Come on now. We really need to get going."

They were in the restaurant before Laney was. While waiting, Sterl looked over the contract for the gallery opening. They wanted a minimum of ten paintings, and would take up to twenty if he had them. Right now, he had seven that he was finished with, and two more that he was working on. The one of the faerie was his favorite by far. He thought of it now. Just thinking of it made him feel good, like he was in sunshine all the time.

The queen was standing in an open field. Her gown was of the purest white, with silver lines. But only when you looked at it from a distance. The closer one got to the painting, the more you could see that the color was an illusion, the lines something more.

The dress wasn't made of material either, but of every creature that he could find in the woods. Each line of silver outlined them so that you could make them out when close enough. Some of them animals that hadn't been seen in a long time.

The trees behind her were also made of animals, some of them peeking from branches, others hiding in the leaves. There was a bear in front of an oak tree just staring at the beauty before him. It had taken him hundreds of hours to get it right, and he'd loved every second of it.

"It says here that I must make an appearance for at least half the showing. I wonder why they'd put that in there." Marty told him what she'd found out from the secretary. "Oh. Well I guess I can understand that. But I'd never get lost in gambling and forget about what was going on with my paintings. I mean, I don't even know how to gamble, much less get lost in it."

"Most people would, I suppose. All the glitter and glitz. There, she's coming. I feel so sorry for her. To find out about your family this way, from strangers."

He stood up when Laney was shown to their table.

"I don't know why I agreed to this." She didn't sit right away, but the host clearing his throat had her moving. "I'm sorry. As I was saying. I don't know why I'm here. I haven't had anything to do with Sally Anne or her husband for years. And I know very little about Heather other than what I could find out on my own. My sister and I...we never really got along well."

"I can understand that. She and her husband, Clay, they

179

weren't people that I would want to know either. As I told you before, Heather is in my brother, Randal's, kindergarten class, and he is the one that first noticed something was going on with her. He told the police all that he knew, which, as it turned out, was very little."

The waiter took their orders and left them again. He was impressed that for as stressed as Laney was, she didn't drink. When he asked her if she was all right, she nodded, then shook her head.

"I'm so lost right now. I've been working on trying to find out what I could about Heather and why my stepmother would have turned her over to Sally Anne, but there wasn't much to be found. And Rosemarie—my stepmother's name—she isn't any better than Sally Anne and Clay were. But the drug of choice for our father and Rosemarie was alcohol, and using their fists was the first line of action instead of talking things out. So because of them, I don't drink, take drugs, even the over the counter ones, nor do I get angry about things that I can't control."

"How long have you lived out here?" Laney told them that she'd been living here her whole life. "I didn't realize that you'd not grown up in Ohio."

"My stepmother again. She wanted me and my dad to move out here just after they were married. I was living with my dad then, and Sally Anne was staying with her mother out here. I had no idea until they married that my dad had been having an affair with Rosemarie and they had Sally Anne. It's how we became a blended family. It wasn't great growing up with them...Sally Anne was spoiled, my father gave into her a lot, claiming that she had had a hard life, and Rosemarie never liked me from the start. I think that's when my dad started to become less of a father than he already had been." Marty said she was sorry. "Don't be. The way I look at it, because of them I have money in the bank. I don't have a lot of debt. I also come and go as I please. I've been happy without them around."

"Heather is going to need you." Sterl was sad to see her shaking her head. "Then she'll end up in the system. I'm sorry about that, but my parents are simply too old to care for her, and my brothers are all working too much to take her in. My wife and I came out here for a business reason, and we thought we'd come by to see if we could take you back with us, just to see the little girl. And figure out what you might like to do about her."

He hoped that his parents would forgive him for saying that they were too old, when in fact, they both were as fit as he was. And with the children around, they'd been taking them for walks and such, so it was a way for them to get into better shape as well.

"I can't care for her. I know nothing about her or my family. My stepmother is a bitch, my father a prick. I see them occasionally, but not enough to go out of my way to be around them." Laney looked at him with tears in her eyes. "I would love to take her in. Raise her as my baby sister, but I don't know how."

"Understandable. It is. We've only recently taken on a child that belonged to a very good friend of ours. Without family to help us, I don't know what we'd do. Benson is about a year old, much younger than Heather, but it's a scary thing to have someone depending on you so much." Laney nodded as their food was set in front of them. "But it would help the adoption agency to get her into a better home if you were to come out and sign some paperwork on this."

It was a lie, all of it. She had no reason to come back with them. She could just as easily give up her rights to the child from here. And Sterl had a feeling that she knew that as well. But the longer she sat there, toying with her food, the more he thought she was going to tell them no.

"If I go out there, will I have to pay for anything that they have incurred? I mean, I don't want to sound cold or anything, but over the years, I've given up a great deal to support the two

181

of them. Am I going to have to pay for their funeral? Back rent? Anything that they might owe?" Sterl told her that it had all been taken care of. "By you?"

"My family. We didn't want Heather to have to be burdened with anything if she were adopted out. I don't know what the system would do, but my family and I, we decided that we'd just take care of it for her." Laney nodded. "We can leave in the morning, or even tonight if you wish. We have a plane."

"I know who you are, Mr. Calhoun. I might be a little slow, but I did look you up. Your family is very wealthy." He nodded. "I also know that I don't have to go there to sign anything. Good try, but I'm not stupid."

"None of us thought you were. We were...I guess you could say we were hedging our bets to get you to come out." She nodded and asked not to be lied to again. "I can do that. But Heather does need you. You are the first person she mentioned when we asked her about relatives. And she told us about the cards you sent with money in them."

"All right. I'll go, but I need to be back here in five days. I've applied for personal time for the death of my sister, and I only have five days plus the two I have off. I won't.... When I want to leave, I expect to be able to do so. No questions asked, nor will I be guilted into taking my sister. I won't go without those reassurances."

"You have them." She nodded and played with her food. "When would you like to leave, Laney? Like I said, we can leave here tonight if you wish."

"Yes. Tonight. But I have to talk to my stepmother first. I don't think she knows that Sally Anne is dead. Unless you notified her." He said that they hadn't. "All right. I'll contact her and let her know. You do whatever it is you need to do to get us out of here in a timely manner, please."

She left them there. Sterl looked over at Marty when she

laughed. After asking her twice what was so funny, she patted him on the cheek and dug into her meal as she explained.

"Poor Randal. He's going to have his hands full with this one. And I'm glad that I'll be around to see it. Laney will have him so tied up in knots, he's going to wish he'd never met her. For a while anyway."

Sterl laughed too. This was going to be a blast.

Before You Go...

HELP AN AUTHOR

write a review

THANK YOU!

Share your voice and help guide other readers to these wonderful books. Even if it's only a line or two your reviews help readers discover the author's books so they can continue creating stories that you'll love. Login to your favorite retailer and leave a review. Thank you.

AWARD WINNING, BESTSELLING AUTHOR

Kathi Barton, winner of the Pinnacle Book Achievement award as well as a best-selling author on Amazon and All Romance books, lives in Nashport, Ohio with her husband Paul. When not creating new worlds and romance, Kathi and her husband enjoy camping and going to auctions. She can also be seen at county fairs with her husband who is an artist and potter.

Her muse, a cross between Jimmy Stewart and Hugh Jackman, brings her stories to life for her readers in a way that has them coming back time and again for more. Her favorite genre is paranormal romance with a great deal of spice. You can visit Kathi online and drop her an email if you'd like. She loves hearing from her fans. aaronskiss@gmail.com.

Follow Kathi on her blog: http://kathisbartonauthor.blogspot.com/

www.ingramcontent.com/pod-product-compliance
Lightning Source LLC
Chambersburg PA
CBHW032143170626
46808CB00006B/2346